WRITTEN BY: Dylan Collins Dunbar
EDITED BY: Dylan Collins Dunbar
COVER DESIGN: Ken Blaznek
COVER PHOTO: J.A. Dunbar
BACK COVER PHOTO: Bryan Mitchell

Copyright © 2024 Dylan Collins Dunbar

All rights reserved. No part of this book may be used or reproduced without the written consent of the copyright owner.

jenniferwestwood/dylan.com

FREE CANDY

By Dylan Collins Dunbar

SPECIAL THANKS TO:

DEDD FRED AND MICK MUGGS.

FREDD – YOU MAKE A HECK OF ZOMBIE MY MAN.

MICK – I COULDN'T HAVE DONE THIS WITH OUT YOU.

TABLE OF CONTENTS:

<u>117</u>

Rupert Westin the III looked at himself in the bathroom mirror. He exhaled sullenly, then picked up his toothbrush and began to brush his teeth. Every morning, Rupert woke up, went into the office, received his job for the day, completed said job, and then went home. Each day, he often wondered if he was living out the back label of a shampoo bottle. This mundane lifestyle was starting to get to him. He wanted something else out of his existence. He needed something new. Something to spice things up.

Rupert stood in front of his closet. He stared blankly at the row of black suits that hung from the rack. Even though they were all identical, he still had a hard time picking out which one would fit his mood for the day. After finally making up his mind, he decided today he would go with a red tie. He went with a red tie every day.

"Hello Mr. Westin. How are you this beautiful morning?" he mumbled to himself before he opened his apartment door.

Like clockwork, the old lady who lived across the hall was bending over to pick up her morning paper. She looked up at Rupert and smiled.

"Hello Mr. Westin. How are you this beautiful morning?" she politely asked.

He smiled, locked his door behind him, and continued down the hallway to the elevator. When the doors opened, a man wearing a UPS uniform from the level above him stood there as if waiting for him to arrive. Rupert groaned as he stepped into the elevator.

"Morning buddy, gonna be a beautiful day today. You got any plans this weekend?" the man asked lightheartedly.

"No," Rupert responded.

They both stood there awkwardly after that, waiting for their floor and the doors to open. The man just smiled at Rupert and exited the elevator first. Rupert let the man get ahead of him a few steps before he followed suit.

Once outside, he was greeted by the doorman.

"Morning Mr. Westin. Lovely day today," the man said with a smile.

Rupert just ignored him like he did every day and went about his way to the bus stop.

It wasn't that these people were beneath him. They were. It was, however, the fact that it was exactly the same thing every single day. Maybe a slight variation from time to time. But for the most part, the same. It's like his own personal Ground Hog's day.

Once on the bus, he sat in the same seat as he always did and patiently waited. It was exactly a thirty-minute and forty-eight-second ride to the office. His job required him to take the bus. Management felt that it was the best way for their employees to get to know their "community" more. Besides, it was lower Manhattan and nobody really owned cars in the city.

Once he stepped off the bus, Rupert still had another block to walk before he got to the office. He always stopped by the convenience store that was right across from the bus stop to get his usual shitty coffee and a pack of gum. He let out an impatient sigh as he waited for the young man in front of him.

"Place all the money in the brown bag and don't try anything stupid," the man said to the store clerk as he waved a snub-nosed revolver at him. The man behind the counter nervously opened the cash register and placed all the money in the man's bag with trembling hands.

"Here. Take it. Just don't hurt me and leave," the man said after setting the bag on the counter.

The would-be thief snatched up the bag and ran out the door. The clerk looked up at Rupert, who was growing more impatient by the minute.

"Gee… thanks for the help there buddy," the man said with frustration.

Rupert just tossed the exact change on the counter, turned, and walked towards the exit.

"That's it? You're not even gonna stick around for the cops? Help identify the man that just robbed me at gunpoint?" the man asked.

Without turning around, Rupert just raised his right hand and gave the man the middle finger before exiting the store. After that, he made his way towards the office. Heaven forbid he was late because some little bastard took too long robbing that convenience store.

Rupert stood in the bullpen with the other employees as they all looked up at a giant dry erase board. Every morning management doled out all the employee's work via the "board". This is where everyone learned what their job for the day was.

Blain Bufford stood next to Rupert as they both searched for their names on the board above them. It was management's cruel job to also put all 150 names in random order. It was never in the same order or had any rhyme or reason.

Heaven forbid they made this easy on us, Rupert thought to himself.

"Sweet! 128!" Blain blurted out in excitement.

"Damnit, 117… Again," Rupert responded.

"Oh, it's not so bad," Blain said. "At least you didn't get 99. That gig's the worst."

Rupert didn't even respond. He just shook his head and left the room. Again, he mumbled unpleasantries under his breath. He walked down the hallway to his desk. Once he got there, he just stood and looked at the stack of reports from the previous jobs he had yet to file. All of them the same thing. Every single one of them a 117.

"Fuck my life," he mumbled.

He could overhear his coworkers around him brag with excitement about the jobs they were assigned today. A few of them even high fived each other. He just continued to stand in front of his desk debating whether or not he was going to just run straight towards the window and leap or try and knock out some reports before lunch. It was a tough call, but he chose the latter.

Rupert sat on his lunch break at the bar of a nearby Applebees and blankly stared at his plate of piping hot chicken fajitas. The bartender slid over his fourth Long Island iced tea. She tried to smile at him, but he didn't look up from his plate. The stranger next to him sipped a gin and tonic while watching the highlights from last night's football game.

"I'm better than this," Rupert said.

"Huh? What's that buddy?" the stranger asked.

"You ever stop and think how your life would have turned out if you made different choices?" he asked without taking his eyes off the untouched food in front of him.

"Every day. Every… day," the stranger responded and downed his drink.

"I literally work for Satan. I mean, I really couldn't have a worse boss. And don't get me started on management. They don't give a shit about anyone. They just order us around and expect us to do what they say without question," Rupert rambled.

"I hear yeah, buddy. The guy I work for down at the bank is horrible. Works us to death and never gives us any feedback on whether we are doing a good job or not. Without any praise, it's kinda pointless. I mean, yeah, sure the money's good, but there's no pride in what I do," the stranger responded. The bartender brought him another gin and tonic.

"Exactly! See you get what I'm saying. Without positive reinforcements, there is no pride in what you do. You're just a slave to the machine. But you see, that's what they want," Rupert said as he placed a straw in his Long Island and proceeded to slurp it down in three gulps.

"Damn man. You should probably eat something," the stranger pointed out.

"Bah…" Rupert said with a wave of his hand. "In fact, I gotta get back to work. Gotta knock this job out in time to finish my reports before close of business."

He slowly pulled himself up from his stool and threw a 100 dollar bill on the bar. As he slowly swayed back and forth from the effects of the liquor, he patted the stranger on the back.

"It's nice to talk to someone that gets it. Have a good one, man," he said as he stumbled towards the door.

"What about your food?" the stranger called out.

"Keep it. It will ruin my buzz," Rupert responded as he left the chain restaurant.

"Well, he's interesting," the man said to the bartender as he pulled the plate of untouched fajitas in front of him.

"Yup, he's here every single day," the bartender responded. "Orders the same thing everytime."

Rupert pulled out his ledger from his breast pocket and checked to make sure he had the correct apartment building. Still swaying back and forth from the effect of the Long Islands, he looked up at the fifty-story apartment building and sighed. The address he needed to go to was on the 50th floor.

"Balls… of course, this can't be that easy," he slurred and stumbled into the lobby.

Before heading to the elevator, he looked around to find the restroom. He located it quickly and made a beeline straight for it. Once inside, he walked over to the mirror and turned the faucet on. He took a minute and splashed some cold water on his face. Then he retrieved a small comb from his pocket and ran it through his hair. Slicking it back, he examined it for anything that was out of place.

"I am good at my job." He said to himself in the mirror. "I am the best at my job."

He corrected his tie and brushed off any lint he could see with the palms of his hands. Rupert straightened his pinky ring that had the symbol of a pentagram in the center. He continued to look himself in the eyes.

"Grr. Rawr. Grrr… look at me. Grrr," he said to himself with zero emotion.

"I am good at my job…" He repeated once again.

He let out another heavy groan and left the restroom and walked straight to the elevator. His shoes squeaked annoyingly as he walked, which caused everyone in the lobby to watch him until he vanished inside the elevator.

"The Girl From Ipanema" played over the speakers, which caused him to slowly and cathartically beat his forehead against the back wall of the elevator. It stopped and opened its doors on the 10th floor. A young woman stepped in and awkwardly pressed the button for the 25th floor. Rupert persisted in banging his head on the back wall at a slow pace. The woman tried not to look at him and wished the elevator moved faster.

"117. 117. 117," he repeated to himself between each whack of his head.

The door opened and the woman quickly stepped out of the elevator to leave him to himself for the rest of the ride up to the 50th floor.

"117"... whack. "117"… whack. "117"… whack, he repeated over and over.

The elevator door dinged one last time as it opened up to the 50th floor. Rupert turned around and stepped into the hallway. Once again, he checked his ledger and made sure he had the correct apartment number.

"555. That should be easy enough. Odds on the left and evens on the right," he said as he put his ledger back into his pocket.

When he came to the door labeled 555, he cleared his throat and repeated to himself. "I'm good at my job…" Then he knocked three times on the door.

"Who is it?" a voice yelled from inside.

Rupert sighed.

"Package delivery for Jason Milner," he called back through the door.

A young man opened the door a crack until it was stopped by the security chain and peered through the crack at Rupert.

"Sorry to bother you, but is this Jason Milner?" he politely asked the young man.

"Yes. Do you have a package for me?" the man responded.

"No," Rupert said, as his face changed from a polite smile to something much darker.

Rupert's eyes were now blood red, and his skin was pale white. Blue and purple veins crisscrossed across his skin and jutted out from his temples. His mouth was now filled with enormously sharp teeth as he let out a guttural hiss. In one effortless push, he opened the door, snapping the chain, stepped into the man's apartment, and closed the door behind him.

They both sat facing each other at Jason's kitchen table in his luxury apartment loft. Jason's nose was broken and his left eye had begun to swell as he tried to focus on the thing that now sat across from him. Rupert's mouth now seemed to resemble a bear trap and his long, yellowed, pointed fingernails tapped on the wooden tabletop as he pondered what to say next.

"What… what are you?" Jason asked as he trembled in fear.

Rupert just raised an eyebrow and didn't respond. He just continued to rap his fingers on the table.

"Are you some kind of demon?" Jason asked.

"Something like that, yeah," Rupert responded.

"Why are you here? What do you want?" the man asked with a whimper.

"Man, this is a pretty nice place you have here," Rupert said as he looked around the studio. "Damn! This is way better than where I live. Hell, I can barely afford the 800 square foot place I rent… and man, would you look at that view," he said.

Rupert retrieved a business envelope from the inner pocket of his suit coat and placed it on the table in front of them. He continued to rap his fingernails on the table and look at Jason inquisitively.

"Inside this envelope is your contract. Remember that almost fatal car crash you were in last year?" he asked the frightened man across from him.

"Yes," the man said. "What are you here for? My soul or something?"

"What?" he responded with a pause. "No. that's actually a 263. You are what my company calls a 117."

"I'm confused. I don't remember making any deals," Jason responded. "I remember being in a car wreck and then the doctors at St. Mary's saved my life."

"Okay, let me explain. Please stop me if you get lost," Rupert said. "So when someone prays for a miracle, that prayer goes up into the great beyond and over to what you could consider a giant switchboard. From there, it goes over to something that would resemble a customer call center for some major corporation. After that, it more or less gets answered by either team. Either the people upstairs pick it up… or the people downstairs pick it up."

He paused to see if this was sinking in. Jason just looked at him wide-eyed as blood trickled down from his busted nose.

"The man upstairs does not hear all the prayers that come across his desk. Also, the guy downstairs, my boss, doesn't just steal people's souls. There's a protocol that both sides follow before a prayer gets answered. It really boils down to who answers the phone first. After that, it's up to the prayer advocate to open a case which then leads to a contract," Rupert said while gesturing with his hands.

"Okay. So if I pray to God and ask him to help me get through my day, it could be answered by the man downstairs?" Jason furrowed his brow as he asked the question.

"No. That's a totally different department. The people answering those calls couldn't give a shit. Ninety percent of those go unanswered, by the way. Now stay focused," he said as he pointed one of his fingers toward Jason. The man nodded quickly while he tried to wipe blood from his nose and mouth with his shirt.

"Okay, where was I?" Rupert said while he scratched at his chin. "Oh, yeah, so the prayer is either answered by one of two teams. Then it goes through a quick review process. Lots of things are taken into consideration. If you're a bad person, it pretty much goes straight to my team. If you are an over-achieving good person, it goes straight to the top upstairs. If you, however, are in the grey area of maybe or maybe not a dickhead, it goes into a queue and has a 50/50 chance of going to either team. Get me?"

Jason just looked at him. He couldn't believe he was being explained how heaven and hell worked. It was like Corporate America. It was starting to make his head hurt. That also could have been from the blow he took from Rupert when he entered his apartment.

"So when my team picks up the call, they hear it out and see if it's worth handling. Nine times out of ten a miracle is performed which draws up a contract. No, it's not a contract for your soul. That's a different department that handles that… So anywho. The miracle is performed and a contract is written up. The stipulation for the contract is that you do something good with your life. If you don't go full dickhead… it can work out in your favor," Rupert said. "Hey, you mind if I see what's in your fridge? I could use something to drink," he asked his prisoner.

Jason still had a hard time processing what exactly was going on. "Sure, help yourself. I don't have a choice, do I?" he asked.

"Not really…" Rupert responded and walked over to his refrigerator. He opened it and pulled out a flavored seltzer water. "Oh cool. I haven't had this flavor before. I do like watermelon."

He cracked open the can and took a long, satisfying drink. Spilling half the contents down his chest because he didn't have any lips.

"Shit. I always forget about that," he said as he looked for something to wipe off his shirt and tie.

"Paper towels are on top of the fridge," Jason said as he pointed toward them.

"Thanks. Okay, where was I?" Rupert asked as he walked back over to the table and sat down.

"You said as long as someone doesn't go full dickhead," Jason responded.

"Right. Okay, so if you don't go full dickhead in your lifetime, you're good. The contract stays valid. If you don't. Well… you void your contract," he replied. This time he took a more careful drink from the can so he didn't spill it all over his lap.

"This is where we get to you, Jason," Rupert said in a more serious tone. "See, someone prayed for you to survive a crash that should have killed you. So by some 'miracle', the doctors over at St. Mary's were able to not only revive you but perform reconstructive surgery."

He reached over to the envelope and pulled out the contents. After unfolding the piece of paper, he pushed it over in front of Jason. Retrieving a pen from his inside pocket, he clicked it with his thumb and set it down on top of the contract.

"You see? After you got out of the hospital, you called your lawyer and decided to sue the family of the woman you hit and killed," he said while giving a shame-shame finger gesture. "You do know the accident was your fault, right? That your blood alcohol level was well beyond the legal limit?"

Jason's mouth seemed to drop as he listened to the thing across from him explain his bleak situation to him. He could feel a sob trying to claw its way out of his throat.

"Your rich parents paid a lot of money to make the police report go away. Then your lawyer took that family for everything they had. You left them with nothing. See Jason. You went full dickhead," Rupert said, then took another swig from his seltzer.

Jason's face began to grow more pale with every word that came out of this thing's mouth.

"You meat bags are pretty much all the same. When given the chance, you get greedy and go full dickhead without a second thought. You could have left the hospital and owned up to what you did. Maybe even donate some money to the family you ruined. Or even set up a charity in that poor woman's name that you killed. Nope. You took the settlement money and bought this place here. All you do is sit around get high and play video games. I mean, that's all fun and all, but you're the current problem with the human race. Just one more greedy, selfish meat bag the world would be better off without," he said with a wicked grin.

"So… so does this mean I'm going to hell?" Jason asked as his eyes began to tear up.

"Different department. Most likely yes. Though seeing how my boss is a fair guy, he always likes to give people one last chance. So, this is going to happen in one of two ways. You are going to either take that pen and sign off your contract to me and then I take back what we gave you. Or I pretty much kill you and then you most certainly will burn in hell. Again, like I said, that's a different department and I can only speculate on that," Rupert said with a polite smile. Which looked extremely awkward, having no lips.

"Take back what we gave you?" Jason asked in an unsettling tone. He nervously fidgeted in his seat as he waited for Rupert to respond.

"Yup. So basically if you sign over the contract, I'm going to take back what the doctors miraculously fixed." He pulled out his ledger and made sure he had the right information before he said anything further. "Right. So I am going to pull off your left arm and your left leg at the hip. After that, I will take off your right leg from the knee down and it says here you will owe us a kidney and a spleen." Rupert said as he referred to his little book.

"Oh God," Jason said as he sobbed.

"Relax. You will pretty much have a 50/50 chance to live. I'll even put on some soothing music. Do you like Hall and Oates?" he asked, then continued. "After I take back what's ours, I'll then place a call to EMS and let them know I have a 117. Once they hear that code, they will be over post-haste. If I had to guess, I'd say they would be here within five minutes. Well, maybe a little longer cuz you're the dingus that decided to move to the top floor of this building." He gave a long pause and looked at Jason directly in the eyes.

"You're only other choice is a slow death. Trust me, my office makes me take my time and make it extra excruciating. So if I were you, I would pick up that pen and sign on the dotted line," Rupert said as he tapped his jagged fingernail on the paper in front of Jason.

"So… what happens after I sign? I mean, if I live?" Jason asked while he wiped tears from his eyes with his forearm.

"Oh. Well, it's simple. You get one last chance to not be a dickhead. Sure you will be a cripple… Jeez, can I even say that word anymore? Cripple I mean? Is that even PC these days?" Rupert asked while he got off topic.

Jason looked at the pen and slowly picked it up in his right hand. He paused for a second, took a deep breath and sniffled. Rupert just watched him while he tapped his fingers on the tabletop. Jason slowly signed his name legibly on the dotted line and then dropped the pen and began to sob uncontrollably.

"Perfect. Now let's get started," Rupert said as he clasped his hands together.

Private Eyes by Hall and Oates seemed to start playing out of nowhere from Jason's stereo as Rupert stood up and walked toward him.

"This will hurt… a lot," Rupert hissed.

ARMAGEDDON GAME

The sun bathed Central Park in a soft blanket of warmth. Families gathered and greeted each other with laughter. A mother played with her two children on a gorgeous Sunday afternoon. They giggled and played games with a bright red Frisbee. Tossing it back and forth to each other while they enjoyed their time together.

Two old friends sat at a table playing chess. They studied the board, strategizing their next move and anticipating the opponent's counter-move. One man was dressed in a black suit and wore a long white beard and had shoulder-length white hair. The other man wore a white suit and had a tightly trimmed beard and black hair that was slicked back with silver feathering his temples. Both of them appeared to be in their mid-60s.

Next to the man in white stood a short, younger man with a somber scowl on his face. His facial features were those of a fighter who had spent a lot of time in the ring. He wore a black suit and had a shaved head.

A tall Nordic-looking man stood next to the man in black. His hair was long and blonde and he wore a gray suit. He carried a look of indifference as if he couldn't really care about the game the two in front of him were playing.

The two men locked in battle had been friends for many years. Every year, on the same date, they met up to play this game of chess and catch up on life. They seemed to have lost count of how many years it had been since they started this tradition. They also had long forgotten how many times the man in black had won.

"Knight takes Pawn," the man in black said as he moved his piece accordingly.

As he watched one of his pawns being removed from the board, the man in white responded, "Damnit."

"How's the kids?" The man in black asked.

"Oh, they are good. I mean a little too ambitious and think they can take over the world," the man in white answered and glowered up at the young man standing next to him.

"They're just tenderfoots. They will come into their own before you know it," he replied. "Rook takes Knight."

"Damn… nice move," the man in white said. "How about you? How's Junior?"

"Doing good I guess. We rarely talk these days," the man in black responded. He reached into a coat pocket and pulled out a cigarette tin. He opened it up, removed a cigarette, and placed it in his mouth. The man then retrieved an obnoxious Zippo lighter that had an American Flag design all over it.

"You know those will kill you," the other man pointed out.

The man in black just raised an eyebrow and lit his cigarette.

"Sorry, knee-jerk reaction," he replied to the man in black's facial expression. "Seriously, though, where the heck did you get that lighter? Oh, by the way… Knight takes Rook."

"What? This thing?" The man in black flicked the Zippo open and closed a few times. "I snagged it at a truck stop on I-10 somewhere between Louisiana and Texas."

"Wait… wait a minute. You of all people… go to truck stops? Aren't they like… well… beneath you?" The man in white questioned.

"Yeah," he responded with a chuckle. "I just love stopping at truck stops. Never know what you will find. You can get everything from snacks and trinkets to a suit of armor. I kid you not... Shit, have you ever been to a Buc-ee's? Those places are hideously massive."

"Afraid not," the man in white responded. He reached over and took a French press filled with freshly brewed coffee and poured some into a cup then handed it to his friend. Then he poured himself a fresh cup and slowly took a sip. Taking a moment to relish the taste.

"This is the best coffee you have ever brought us," the man in black said as he set his cup down on the table. "What kind is it again?"

"It's Ethiopian Harrar," the man in white responded. "It's a nice balanced light blend from a roaster right over here in Soho. Did you know it's a common misconception that the darker the roast, the stronger the coffee is? I mean, the more caffeine it has." He paused while looking at the board with increased concentration. "That's not true. The lighter the roast, the more caffeine it has."

"I didn't know that. I really like it. Please bring it next time. Knight takes Pawn," the man in black said.

"Damnit. Okay, hold on, let me think here," he responded. "Ha! Bishop takes Knight!"

"Nice move," the man in black said while he took a drag from his cigarette. "Rook takes Bishop."

"Hell's fire! Nice one," the man in white said while studying the board. "Hey, I've always been meaning to ask you something."

The man in black took another sip of coffee. "Go ahead, ask me anything you want. Pawn takes Knight, by the way."

"Crap," the man in white whined. "Okay, I've always wanted to know this. Say you are stranded on a desert island."

They both paused and looked at each other.

"Okay... 'try' and imagine you are stranded on a desert island. What album would you take with you to listen to? You can only pick one." The man in white asked while taking another drink of coffee.

"That's easy. Miles Davis's 'Kind Of Blue'," he replied while taking a drag.

"Are you shitting me? I never figured you as a jazz guy. I mean, that's supposed to be my thing. Right?" The man in white asked.

"Yeah," the man in black said with a husky chuckle. "It's a great album though. Bishop takes Rook."

"I'm more of a 'Bitches Brew' kinda guy. But yeah, that is a great album. Good call," the man in white said as he paused to contemplate his next move. "Bishop takes Bishop."

"Nice one," he responded. "Okay. How about you? What's your desert island album?"

"That's a hard one," the man in white stopped to ponder. "I would have to go with White Lion's second album 'Pride'."

"For real?" The man in black said with confusion. "Pawn takes Bishop."

"Oh yeah. Totally underrated band of the 1980s. They were way ahead of their time. Besides, I feel that Vito Bratta's guitar solo in the song 'Wait' is the greatest rock and roll guitar solo of that era," The man in white said with excitement.

"Let me guess. You had something to do with that, didn't you?" The man in black asked after taking another drag and crushing out his cigarette.

The man in white just gave a bashful shrug. "Maybeeee…"

They could tell their game was coming to an end. Both men sat there with crinkled brows as they intensely studied the board that sat in front of them. After a long and quiet ten minutes, the man in white's face turned into a smile and he seemed to beam with pride.

"Will you look at that?" he said with excitement. With his right hand, he slowly moved his queen into place, making sure his move was correct. "My friend, I believe that's checkmate."

"Well, I'll be damned," the man in black replied while he scratched his chin. "You finally did it. You finally beat me."

"Jeez, how many years has it been? I lost count," the man in white said as he rubbed his hands together in delight.

"Yeah, it's been eons," the man in black said as he looked at the tall man standing next to him, who only groaned in response.

The man in white turned and looked at the short man next to him. "You may begin, Damian."

Damian retrieved a cellphone from his inside suit pocket and began to send out a text message. After he pressed send, he placed the phone back in his pocket.

"It is done my liege," the man said.

"Delightful," the man in white said with a wicked grin.

In the background, missiles could be seen breaking free of the horizon and treetops of Central Park. The sounds of warning sirens began to wail and fill the air. Those people in the park who were once enjoying their day now began to panic. The mother grabbed up her two children and began to run for safety, leaving the Frisbee behind. Some of them immediately went for their cell phones. Others just watched the sky as others ran for their lives. As the pandemonium increased, the man in black just looked at the man across from him.

"Seriously?" He said with an annoyed look. "You couldn't be more original?"

"What?" the man in white responded. "Why should I do all the work when these apes have the means to do it themselves?" He shrugged.

The man in black shook his head. "Couldn't you have gotten Godzilla or even a zombie plague or something else? Anything but this. It's so… 1980s."

Moments later, the first missile hit the coastline of NYC. In the distance, a massive mushroom cloud erupted towards the heavens. Another one followed after that. Then another.

"Hey, man. You do you and I'll do me. Besides, we have to get going. I'm expecting quite a line piling up at my front gates soon," said the man in white as he slapped his hands on his knees like a typical mid-westerner and stood up.

"Actually…I think I'm gonna take one last walk before we head home," the man in black responded.

"As always, it's a pleasure, my friend. Now, since I won, I get to choose the game next time," he said while clapping his hands. "I hope you like Yahtzee. Until next time, amigo."

The man in white straightened his tie and nodded to the Nordic man to his friend's left. Then he turned around and walked off into the cloud of smoke that was beginning to rush towards them, engulfing the entire park and destroying everything in its path. Damian followed behind his father.

The man in black stood up, sighed, and turned to his friend.

"What?" he asked the Norde.

"You did that on purpose, sir," the man responded.

"Oh, don't stand there and tell me this world didn't need a hard reset, Michael," the man in black said as they both began to walk off in the opposite direction as the man in white.

They both slowly strolled through the park as it turned to ash. The once majestic skyline was instantly reduced to rubble. Burned bodies and fragments of the previous world now surrounded them. Michael turned to the man in black with a tired look like they had been here before.

"So you've done the giant lizards and then the talking apes. Do you have any plans for what you will do this time?" he asked.

"Cats, Michael. I think I'll do something with cats," the man in black said as both walked off through the cinders that was once called New York City.

SHITBIRDS AND APPLESAUCE

It was 1969, and we had just spent an entire month straight in the rain. Around this time, good ole' Nixon was starting to order massive amounts of US troops to withdraw from the war. We were not one of the lucky ones. They stationed me and the boys in North Vietnam and had new orders for us to clear a patchwork of tunnel systems. The higher-ups had believed that the VC were up to something nasty and we had to go behind enemy lines and scout a few tunnels looking for intel. The Cu Chi tunnels were the definition of claustrophobia. They also helped the little bastards master guerilla warfare. Allowing them to keep popping up out of nowhere, then disappearing just as quickly. We learned they were using tunnels to act as trapdoors for sneak attacks. Once the rain finally stopped, they gave me and the boys the green light and we went in.

My names Fred, and with all this crazy stuff going on in the news today about a virus outbreak, it took me back. I saw some reports talking about people going mad and attacking each other. I know exactly what's going on. Ever since that night in 69, I've been waiting for this day to come.

Been through all this already. Back in the war. On a much smaller scale, of course, but I've seen this before. I've been right there face to face and shit deep in 'em. Can't reason with 'em. Can't shock and aw 'em. Can't scare 'em. You best not hesitate either or you risk getting infected. Only one way you can put 'em down. That's the head. Gotta get 'em in the head, but I digress.

I figured it would be wise to write down my story so that someday someone might read this and learn that this wasn't a random act. This has been something those commie bastards have been planning for years. I know because I saw the files and reports firsthand.

In June of 1969, we lost a lot of good men. Some of those heroes… were my friends.

Me and the rest of my platoon from the First Air Calvary had cleared the area and located the tunnel system. We torched everything. We had done this sort of thing before and my boys were well equipped to handle the situation.

I was going to head a three-man team into the first system. Wasn't smart to bring any more than that. It was gonna be cramped down there and the fewer men with guns up my ass, the better.

I always took Private Rudy Dunn and Private Sisco Tavaris. Rudy was a college football player from Saint Louis, Missouri. He was a running back who stood only 5'8" but weighed 203 lbs of solid muscle. His jersey number was twenty. So the boys nicknamed him D20. Sisco Tavaris was a 5'5" Hispanic from Brooklyn, New York. He had the temper and bullheadedness to match. Whatever the circumstance, I loved having my little Mexican jumping bean with me. Oh, I know I can't say that anymore, but I didn't mean nothin' by it and, of course, it was 1969. A lot has changed since then. Anyway, once you set Tavaris on a task, he would never stop till it was done.

Private Tavaris cleared the debris and opened the makeshift hatch. All three of us tunnel rats climbed in head first. One pair of lips to one man's puckered asshole.

You never know how massive these systems are going to be. Couldn't just toss down a grenade and be done. These were not bunkers. These were usually an intricate labyrinth of zigs and zags and the occasional command room or storage room. They had supplies, food, and ammo. It was another world down there.

My men and I did this a lot during the Tet Offense in 68. The three of us were a well-oiled machine. We got in and we got out. Killed anything and everything. We took whatever we thought looked important. Maps, photos, files, orders, and anything else that told us what these little bastards were up to.

We cleared the first set of tunnels pretty quickly. We only had to slit a few throats and snatched up a few maps with writing on them. Just in and out without a scratch. As I said, we were a well-oiled machine.

The second set, however, is where it all got FUBAR.

We dropped down into the second set of tunnels. Rudy had a silenced .38 caliber revolver he brought along. It's not like the movies. Those suppressors don't completely silence the shot. They do drastically make it somewhat bearable in the super tight quarters of the Cu Chi systems.

Sisco and I only used our knives for the most part. If the shit hit the proverbial fan. I had my Remington 870 12-gauge pump. I had her sawed off at about 17 inches. I liked to keep her handy for close encounters. Sisco had the standard sidearm, which was a 1911. In most tunnels, Rudy would probably fire a handful of times and we would only have to use our knives in a few instances. Like I said, we were fast and clean.

The second system dropped us right off into a hornet's nest. Five North VC troops were standing around a table yelling at each other. We just happened to stumble in, and Rudy took them all out in a flurry of shots. It was like he was shooting fish in a barrel.

There was no telling how many other VCs heard those shots, but we knew someone probably did. So we picked up the pace and continued through the tunnels.

After a series of lefts and rights and more lefts and more rights, we came into another room. This room was different. The walls were covered with diagrams of the human body. Documents and photographs were scattered all over the table. Most of the reports were in Vietnamese. There were a few, however, that were in Russian. The place resembled a makeshift laboratory of some kind.

Those people that were inside them photographs looked infected. But infected with what? We didn't know just yet. They reminded me of the photographs I had seen of the Nazi death camps from WWII. The people in the photos did not look right. It's like their eyes were void of life. We figured all of this was in the "important" column, so we bagged it all up and continued our way through the system.

More lefts and rights as we inched our way deeper. We slowed our pace down a bit. Sensing things could get weird. At least we were smart enough to "try" and be careful. Having an all out shit storm down here was not at the top of our list of things to do. Plus, Private Tavaris was reigning poker champion back at base camp, but tonight I was gonna knock him off that high horse.

We finally came to a split in the tunnel system. Tavaris naturally took the tunnel to the right and scouted ahead while I took the tunnel to the left and Rudy watched the tunnel we just came from.

We both would go in about 20 yards and then report back with what we saw. From there, the three of us would make the call of which tunnel to hit first. Rudy would then set a little booby trap for anyone that came in behind us. If or when we had to backtrack, Rudy would just disarm it.

When I got back I noticed that ole Tavaris hadn't returned. Rudy told me he heard some ruckus, and he believed he heard him cuss right before I returned. So right then and there we picked the right tunnel. Rudy set a claymore and a trip wire for some sorry bastard and off we went.

We found Tavaris. He was about 25 yards in. He just sat there on the floor with a blank look on his face. There was the body of a Russian soldier lying in the center of the tunnel. His head was caved in.

Tavaris had told us that he snuck up on the Russkie. Slit his throat, but the prick wouldn't seem to die. When he grabbed the soldier from behind to pull the man off balance, he took a bite of Tavaris's forearm. After his throat was slit. He told us that blood went everywhere, and the guy kept comin' at him. He stabbed him a few times and even then, he still wouldn't go down. To make one last effort not to use his sidearm, he pulled out his shovel and bashed the Russian's head in. That's when he said he stopped moving.

Tavaris told us the man's features were just all wrong. He resembled the subjects we saw in the photos we gathered up back at the makeshift laboratory. The Russian also didn't seem to make any audible noises other than moans and grunts.

"Aw shitbirds and applesauce," I said.

The laceration on Tavaris's arm was already getting pretty nasty. So we quickly cleaned it and wrapped it up. He gave us both the thumbs up and insisted we press on. We all knew something was going on down here and we needed to find out more information before we got the hell out of dodge.

We quietly crept deeper into the maze. It was odd because we heard no radio chatter or voices echoing through the system in front of us. Normally, this would have eased our nerves, but for some reason, with everything we just discovered, this made it worse. Tensions rose and imaginations ran wild.

Was the VC conducting experiments down here with the help of the Russians? Were the Russians using the Viet Cong as test subjects for some new Cold War virus? Did we just walk into a Soviet biological weapons experiment? All these thoughts seemed to run rapidly, like a pissed-off bull in a china shop through all corners of my head.

Since we were behind enemy lines and down in the bowels of the Ci Chu system, none of us dared speak. We just focused on completing the mission. Which was to see what the fuck was going on down here and gather what intel we could and get the hell out. Once out, we were gonna erase these tunnels from the planet and whatever remained inside.

For the next few minutes, it was smooth sailing. Then we happened upon a small communication room. The radio looked like it had been destroyed with an axe. It was clear that someone didn't want whatever was down here leaving or calling for backup.

I was beginning to regret letting Rudy smoke the VC we first ran across when we entered the tunnel. We really should have interrogated them or brought one of them back top side. They were the only living things we saw in the tunnel that night. Well, "were" living.

I could tell that Private Tavaris wasn't doing so well. He was starting to sweat and he was moving a little slower than usual. We should have gotten our asses out of there as soon as he encountered the Russian. If we had known then what we know now, I would have just called in a bombing raid and been done with it. Should have napalmed the entire place to Kingdom Come.

We only went another 20 or 30 yards in when we entered another room. This room looked like it was a commander's office. Even though it was just a hole cut out of Vietnamese dirt, it had a commanding officer's vibe. For example, in the center sat a large wooden table. At that table sat a man who looked like he was wearing a general's uniform. His mouth just drooped open, and he looked right at us.

Two Russian soldiers were bent over the man's left and right clavicles as they slowly gnawed away at either side of his throat. Blood had run down his uniform and covered most of the table. The man was obviously dead, but his eyes still looked right through us.

"Jesus," Rudy muttered out loud.

That's when the crunching and slurping noises stopped. Both of them Russkies looked up at the same time.

And that was my first encounter with a Zed Head. A fuckin' zombie. Real-life walkin' dead. To this day, I still see those Russian bastards in my dreams. Chewing and slurping away at that dead general. Still makes this old army vet's skin crawl.

They both looked at us with milky, dead eyes. One of them was missing half his face like it had been gnawed off or something. The other was missing an eye and had what looked like a pencil sticking out of it. Gore ran down their chins in gobs like a toddler that just ate a bowl of chocolate pudding and used their hands. The only sound they made was a soft moan as they slowly shambled around the table.

"Jesus shitballs these assholes are slow," I said as I motioned to Rudy to take them out.

Rudy shot one in the chest with his .38. A little mist of blood-spattered as the bullet entered the one-eyed bastard's chest. That should have dropped the fucker right there if he were alive.

I pulled out my Remington and blasted the same one in the chest with buckshot. The momentum caused him to step backwards a couple of steps but it didn't put him down. He just kept slowly walking towards us.

It wasn't 'til Rudy walked up point blank and put one in its head did it fall. Dropped like a sack of potatoes. Tavaris took out his .45 and shot the second one in his head for the same reaction.

"What the fuck are these?" Rudy spat.

We didn't know what to call these things at first. Zombie wasn't exactly an everyday word back then. I did think it was a major coincidence that George A Romero released his famous movie later that year. Which I found hard to watch and thought it was tame compared to the real thing.

"What's the plan, Sarge?" Tavaris asked.

I honestly wasn't quite sure what our next move should have been. I wonder that if things had gone differently down there, would all this have snowballed fifty-five years later?

Tavaris was hurt badly, and I could tell. He would have followed Rudy and me to the ends of the earth and back. So I ordered us to turn around and get the hell outta there and take the intel we had and cut our losses. I wanted to complete the mission, but I also wanted to save my men. It's a heavy burden going into war with people under you that you are responsible for. So much from this night haunts me to this day. We should have got out once we gathered what we did from the laboratory and maybe… just maybe a few more soldiers would have made it home that year.

"We need to get the hell outta here. The brass needs to see this intel ASAP," I said. "We need to get Tavaris looked at and make sure he's okay."

The boys agreed. We gathered up whatever paperwork was scattered all over the general's table, some of which was covered in his blood, and we turned around and began to quicken our pace back toward the way we came.

Right then we heard our cleverly placed claymore trap go off.

The explosion sent tremors through the entire system, causing dirt to fall on our heads from the ceiling. Once our ears stopped ringing, we hauled ass back and hoped the tunnel was still intact. It wasn't.

"Shitbirds," I said once we saw what was ahead of us.

The tunnel had collapsed from the explosion, burying whatever tripped it and also blocking us from getting out the way we came in.

"Looks like this ain't the way, boys," I said and motioned everyone to go back the way we came.

These tunnel systems always have multiple ins and outs. We just had to go deeper into the belly of the beast to find it. Eventually, we would find an exit. I just hoped we got Tavaris medical attention fast. His face under the lamplights of the tunnels was looking worse. He now looked jaundiced. Little did I know at the time that he was already dead.

"What if we run into more of those things?" Tavaris asked.

"Go for the head and pray," Rudy responded.

"Keep in mind these things are slow as tar. I bet we can run past them or even take them out with our knives. Just be careful. Tavaris's appearance here suggests that their bites can cause an infection of some kind," I said.

I should have shot my friend in the head right there. Hindsight is

20/20 though, right?

We hauled butt like we were late for prom. The three of us back-tracked with ease. We passed the general's makeshift quarters and continued into the system. Deeper and deeper we went, without any signs of life or a way out. We knew if we kept on, we would eventually find some kind of trapdoor leading to the surface.

It took us hours to locate a way out. The time down there felt like it moved slower than normal. What took hours seemed to feel like days. It didn't help that we had to stop every thirty minutes or so for Tavaris to catch his breath. Once we found the ladder that led us to the way out of that hellhole, we heard a scream from deeper in the tunnel. Really, it was more like an angry shriek than a scream.

"What the hell was that?" Rudy said as he helped push Tavaris up the ladder.

"No time to find out. Move your asses," I spat back.

We heard it scream again. This time, we could tell it was closer. We didn't want to get trapped down there with a sick Tavaris and up close and personal to whatever else was down here. As experienced as we were at what we did, I could tell we were all starting to question a lot of our life's decisions at this moment.

It's amazing how fast you can move through a small tunnel system when everything goes to shit. When Tavaris reached the trapdoor, he carefully swung it open. A deluge of rainwater came pouring down on us. It had begun to rain again like it did every damn day. At that moment, we had no idea how long we were down there or how long it had been raining. So we crawled our way out and through the mud and closed the trapdoor behind us. We heard one last screech as it slammed shut.

We got to our feet, and we were back in the jungle. Took us a minute to check our surroundings. We didn't wanna walk in on a VC patrol. That would have been like climbing out of an oven and into oncoming traffic. We followed our compass south. By now, we had to help Tavaris. He was not able to walk on his own anymore.

God, I wish I had shot him.

I was just a snot-nosed kid from Wichita, Kansas. I was only twenty years old. What did I know about giving orders that got men killed?

We went south 'til we started seeing some landmarks we recognized. Don't ask me what they were because to this day I don't remember.

We finally made it back to where the rest of our platoon was stationed. They were still holding the entrance area of the tunnel system. We were also lucky we didn't get our heads blown off by friendly fire.

When we got back to base camp, they took Tavaris to medical right away. God, I wish I had shot him. A medic gave Rudy and me a quick once over and then we were off to talk directly to command. We debriefed them and gave them the intel we found. They were going to go back with a full-scale assault on that section of the Cu Chi system and the surrounding areas.

Rudy and I were to take Sisco, once he was cleared, to Saigon in the morning. We were to return to base and discuss what we saw directly with the top brass. None of that actually happened, though. Because at about 0300 hours, all hell broke loose when Tavaris went apeshit.

He started by attacking two nurses and killing them. Ate half their faces off to be exact. Then, shortly after that, the nurses changed. Once the dead nurses rose, Tavaris had already made his way over to the barracks.

Those poor kids didn't even stand a chance. The majority of the soldiers in those barracks were newbies that had just arrived that day. It was like "Here, welcome to war… now goodnight and enjoy your deaths."

It didn't take long for a dozen Zed Heads to be chewing their way through base camp. Rudy and I went to work. We didn't stop to help anyone or gather more men. We just knew what we were up against and just went to work. Our major priority was to neutralize the threat and keep those that aren't dead yet… not dead.

We moved methodically together, and we worked like a symphony. Rudy would either clip them in the head with his .38 or I would knife them under the chin. We moved fast. They were already dead, and we didn't want to be. So we had the edge.

Before we found Tavaris, we both halted at the sound of a familiar shriek from outside the camp.

The newbie soldiers ran around screaming like kids. Bodies of their brothers in arms eatin' to death or turned into zombies.

The shriek from off in the jungle seemed to make everyone stop for a split second. As if everyone heard it at once and shit their pants. I can't lie. That sound made my asshole pucker too.

Whatever was down in those tunnels found us. We have no idea how the hell it did that because we were hundreds of miles away. Must have run all through the day and all through the night to have gotten here by now. It didn't matter how it got here. All that mattered was that it "was" here.

That's when we found Tavaris. He was hunched over a fresh corpse of a newbie. He was just munching away like he hadn't eaten in a decade. Gnawing and crunching. That kid might still be alive if I just shot my friend when I had the chance.

I'll never forget that look in his eye when he saw Rudy and I. That look of emptiness. Nothing that was Private Sisco Tavaris was there anymore. It was just a primal beast that was relentless for the taste of human flesh. So, I shot him in the face with my 1911.

My .45 caliber bullet struck him just above his right eye. The force caused his eyeball to explode as a giant hole ripped through his forehead. The shell of our friend and brother fell straight to the ground.

I will never forgive myself.

Well, as soon as we were done standing around feeling sorry for ourselves, we had to get our asses in gear. The sirens were blaring all hell's bells. Men were running all over the place. It was a complete shit show.

Once the Army learned that shooting them in the head worked, they quickly got to neutralizing the situation. It wasn't going to take them long to get it somewhat under control.

Rudy and I did not stick around long enough to see exactly how it went down. We had to take care of something. Whatever was down in the tunnel system had somehow tracked us down at great lengths and clearly wasn't happy.

With the shit still hitting the fan at the base, we made our way towards where we last heard the screams. The jungle lit up like a Christmas tree behind us as the neutralizing of the undead commenced. Once our eyes adjusted, we were off. Rudy was armed with his pistol and a bowie knife, and I had my shotgun and sidearm.

The scream was getting closer. Much faster than I had liked. So we decided to stop and hold our ground. I took a knee and held my boomstick up to my shoulder. Rudy stood behind me with his pistol aimed in front of us.

"Don't fire until I do," I whispered.

We heard the scream and guessed it couldn't have been more than fifty yards in front of us. We kept calm and held our ground. Then the next scream came from our right.

The sky behind us exploded like the Fourth of July. With that light, we could make out movement that was now behind us. Then we heard the scream to our left, and it was much closer. Both Rudy and I pivoted.

Whatever this thing was, it was stalking us. This was not your typical dimwitted Zed Head. This was a predator.

We heard it running at us before we heard it scream. It came at us from our six o'clock. I spun and blasted it right in the gut with buckshot. It bounced back up just as fast as it hit the ground. Asshole came at us a second time.

Whatever this was. It wasn't your typical undead. He wore a Russian uniform that had been shot full of holes. His face was similar to a Zed Head. It was gaunt and jaundiced like the others. This one, however, was twisted into something rabid. This thing was pissed, and it showed. You could tell its mind was working in a primitive sort of way.

Rudy was able to clip off two rounds before it barreled into us.

Apparently, Rudy missed.

This new Super-Zed Head tossed me aside and pounced on Rudy. Well, more like Rudy's Bowie knife. He twisted and turned his massive knife and lifted the thing off the ground with both hands. Blood poured down Rudy's chest.

The thing also had its teeth latched onto his left shoulder. Finally, it let go and just snapped its teeth at the air before Rudy tossed it off his knife. He tossed him a good five yards. With him came a spray of Rudy's blood. It all happened so fast that I didn't realize that Zed was able to make contact with Rudy's throat once more before he tossed him.

Rudy fell to his knees and held his hands to his neck.

The Russian lept up again and rushed at me this time. I was able to pepper his lower left jawbone. More or less winged him. But took a good chunk. The blast took the pep outta his step for a minute. Just long enough for me to turn to attend to Rudy. Before I could get a word out of my mouth. Rudy placed his revolver to his temple and pulled the trigger.

It was like it all happened in slow motion. It's still hard not to get choked up at what he had done. He had just shown the single most act of bravery I had ever witnessed to this day. There is no telling how many lives he saved by taking his own life.

I had to keep my head in the game as this son of a bitch had now officially killed the last of my team. I remember screaming at the top of my lungs as I wracked shell after shell into this abomination. Finally, I hit him with my last shot right in his forehead. He dropped and slid past me in the mud and tall grass.

I just stood there breathing. Couldn't believe what the last 24 hours had brought me. The gunshots back at the base had died down. Wouldn't you know it that it started to rain. Again.

Once the mess was cleaned up. I told the brass about the dead super zombie thing. I told them that it was a good 100 yards from the base. That it would be the Russian one missing most of its head. Told them about Rudy Dunn and Sisco Tavaris. Those two men and I had seen our fair share of shit for the three years we were stationed together.

Not only did I lose good friends and great soldiers that day, I felt like I lost family. You don't spend that much time together deep in the shit bowels of hell and not become that close.

After they checked me out and made sure I wasn't bitten, they immediately sent me back to Saigon to debrief some serious higher-ups. There I sat, in a large room filled with officers and bureaucrats. There were also a few guys in suits with sunglasses. I guessed them to be CIA or some form of spook operation. The room was so tense you could shit a diamond.

I told 'em everything. Told them about what it was we found down in the tunnels. How just a simple bite seemed to be what spread this, whatever it was. Also, I made sure to point out that shooting them in the head seemed to do the trick.

I talked for a good thirty minutes. None of them said a thing to me. They all just patiently waited for me to finish. Once I finished, they all just stared at me. Finally, one of them spoke up.

"We are going to need you to sign these disclosure forms." The one who introduced himself as General Antilles said.

Can you believe that? You go through hell and all they want you to do is sign some paperwork that says you legally can't tell anyone else about it. After that, I received the Medal of Honor and they gave me an honorable discharge.

I was sent home, where I had to try to adapt back to normalcy. It took me a while to get my shit straight, but I did it. Even eventually got a good security job with a car company called MoGo Mato Motors.

So today all over the news channels everything is once again FUBAR. I figured the hell with the government's paperwork. Don't know who will find this, but I'm sure someone will, eventually.

So if you are reading this, I am sure the world is either about to end or it already has. This was an act of war gone wrong. I am sure this virus, or whatever it was, was designed to be dropped behind enemy lines and let it do its thing.

The big question is: "Whose enemy lines?"

FREE CANDY

You know what's wrong with the world today? People just don't like clowns anymore, Herbert Richards thought to himself as he drove his late 1980s Ford Econoline through Yoctangee Park in downtown Chillicothe, Ohio. The van's brakes squealed every time he came to a stop as he circled the park, watching for anyone who might be interested in what he had to offer.

It was a hot, humid, unforgiving afternoon. All of which caused the rank sulfuric odor of the local paper mill to be extra pungent in the southern Ohio heat. The AC in his van had not worked for almost a decade now. He always told himself he was going to get it fixed, but just never got around to it. He adjusted the rearview mirror so that he could look at his reflection.

The heat started to make his makeup run down his face. It turned him from a happy clown into what now looked like a very sad clown. He pulled out a white dingy handkerchief and blotted at his face, careful not to smudge his makeup.

Jesus, you know what people don't like more than clowns? Sad ones, he thought as he tried to correct the hot mess that he'd become.

Herbert had not been able to find a good gig in probably seven years now. Being that he was in his late 60s it was getting harder and harder to lure them in. In the 1990s, he was able to hop out just about anywhere, do a little song and dance, maybe a couple of balloon animals, and bam! Just like that, they would be eating out of his hand. It wasn't until around 2010 that he saw a decline in people's attitudes towards clowns. People just didn't respect the art form anymore.

"Fuck it," he muttered as he tossed the handkerchief on the sun-cracked vinyl dash of his van. The serpentine belt whined as he gave it some gas to continue his circling of the park. There had to be someone here for him. Someone had to want what he had.

Yoctangee Park was adjacent to the old historical district of Chillicothe and housed a 12-acre lake. The lake was surrounded by many species of trees such as Honey Locust, London Planes, and various types of Elms. The lake was home to numerous types of ducks that had grown used to being around people.

Those who worked downtown would stroll down on their lunch break with bread or frozen peas and just relax and feed the birds. At one end of the lake was a stone archway bridge that crossed over a small section, making it a landmark people came to see for the city of Chillicothe.

Herbert spotted a group of kids kicking a soccer ball around under a shade tree while their parents watched at a distance from a picnic table. He saw this as his chance and he pulled his van over to a squealing halt. He pulled down the sun visor and looked at himself.

"Okay Buster Brown, here's your chance. Let's bedazzle them like they have never seen before," he said, giving himself a pep talk.

Herbert flung open the driver's side door and proceeded to jump out in an excited, playful manner. Except it didn't go as planned. His left suspender got caught on the door striker, causing him to yank backwards off balance. His momentum kept his lower half going as he flipped up in the air and landed on his back with a loud thud. As the wind evacuated his chest, he lay there and gasped for air while he stared up at the trees above.

The children just pointed and laughed at the elderly clown sprawled out not more than twenty feet in front of them. He landed so hard that his red nose popped off and lay next to him. He looked down once he caught his breath and saw his big red shoes were pointed straight up to the sky like two comedic water skies. The children just continued to laugh.

They are laughing at you, Herbert, he thought to himself.

He just sighed and decided to lay there a while longer. The children's parents called them over to where they were sitting and scolded them for laughing. One woman yelled out to him, asking if he was okay. Herbert just raised his right hand to the sky and gave a thumbs up.

"Little fucking bastards," he muttered as he continued to lie flat.

After another 10 minutes, he swallowed what was left of his pride, stood up, and brushed himself off. Slowly, he climbed back up into his van and closed the door. He sat there for a minute to gather his thoughts. After he mulled it over he figured the best thing for his wounded pride was a stiff drink. He put the van in drive and in a cloud of black smoke and belt squeal he drove off into downtown to hit his favorite watering hole.

Herbert sat at the bar at Steiner's Speakeasy, ordered his third old fashion, and looked like the punchline from a bad joke.

"You hear the one about the clown that walks into a bar?" he said to the bartender.

The bartender looked around, then shook his head no. They were the only two souls in the bar at the moment.

"A clown walks into a bar. The bartender asks… is this some kinda joke?" Herbert then tossed back his drink in one large gulp.

The man just sighed loudly. The clown took the hint and paid his tab and proceeded to walk out the front door. He stepped out onto South Paint Street and walked to his van, which was parked about half a block to the south in the historical district. When he reached the door of his van, he saw his reflection in the window and it finally dawned on him that it was time for a change.

Herbert's makeup looked awful. The lines in his face ran deep and the bags under his eyes were enormous. Was this what rock bottom looked like? Was this the power above telling him that it was time to move on? Did anyone really care anymore? All of these thoughts ran through his head as he stood there. Realizing the golden hour was upon him, he figured he would give it one last try. If he wasn't able to find someone by sundown, he would throw in the towel for good and look for a new way of doing things. He nodded to himself in the reflection, hopped in his van, and sped off back to the park to see what he could muster up.

He once again circled the lake to see what he could find. At this hour, there weren't many people out and about. Just a few teenagers smoking grass and drinking from paper bags. A young couple walked their dog as they looked oddly at an elderly clown slowly driving by in his old beat-up Ford.

Whelp, I can take a hint," he said to himself with a sigh of defeat. Then he saw him. In all his glory. Under the glow of a streetlight stood a 6-year-old boy. He appeared to be lost and crying. The boy had sandy brown spiky hair and held his arms close to his chest as his puffy, tear-filled eyes darted back and forth nervously. Herbert brought his van to a grinding halt and slammed it into park.

Oh boy oh boy oh boy oh boy oh boy, he thought to himself. *Okay buddy, keep it together. We got one chance at this. Don't fuck this up.*

He flung open the van door and hopped out. This time not landing on his ass. He figured it was time to bring out the big guns.

"Hey little guy! Do you like balloon animals?" he belted as he darted from around the front of the van. The boy seemed startled at the sight of a withered old clown in dingy, unflattering clothing and big shoes. Herbert reached into his pocket and pulled out some balloons and proceeded to blow them up. The child just looked at him, confused and terrified. In a hurried, frantic display of twists and squeaks, he twisted the red balloon into the shape of what looked like a dog.

"Look! A dog… What does a dog say, little buddy?" Hubert asked the boy. The child just sniffled and sobbed.

Okay, tough crowd, he thought.

"Bow-wow. Right?" he asked the little boy. He noticed the child was wearing a pair of blue jeans and a black hoodie with some kind of giant Japanese cartoon robot on it.

"How about I make you a robot? Would you like that, kid?" the clown asked.

Without waiting to hear an answer, he retrieved more balloons from his pockets and began to blow them up as quickly as he possibly could. In a mesmerizing attempt to please his audience, he frantically twisted and pulled the balloons into a robot. With his tongue sticking out of his mouth and sweat beginning to bead up on his forehead, he held out his creation in triumph. The boy just looked at him, more confused than before.

"Mister, that looks just like the dog you made," the boy said, looking up at the tattered old man in ridiculous makeup.

"Well shit," he said in response. He tossed the balloon monstrosity aside and knelt down to the boy.

"Where's your parents, kid?" Herbert asked. The little boy wiped a gob of snot bubbles with the forearm of his sweatshirt and shrugged.

"One minute they were here and the next minute they were gone," he sputtered between sobs.

A dark look fell over the clown's face as he smiled at the six-year-old.

"How about we take you back to my place and we figure out how to get in touch with your parents," he said while putting his hand on the child's shoulder. The kid wiped away some tears and nodded his head. Herbert helped the boy over to his van and opened the passenger door. The old clown lifted the child up and placed him in the front seat.

t's not far from here and I have free candy," he said, which caused the child's face to light up at the sound of the word candy. He closed the door hurried around the front of his van, and hopped in. Herbert cranked over the engine and turned on the headlights. Before he put the vehicle into drive, he turned and looked at the boy.

"What's your name, kid?" he politely asked.

"Milton," the boy responded.

The old man nodded, put the van in drive, and headed out of the park. Just as they crossed Main Street and headed down South Paint Street, the boy began to speak. This time, he sounded different. His voice was deeper and more baritone. It no longer remotely resembled the frightened child he found in the park moments ago.

"We've been waiting for you, Herbert," the boy said.

He spun towards the six-year-old boy sitting next to him. Milton sat straightforward as his head turned all the way to his left, staring at Herbert while his van crept along. The old man's stomach cramped up and the hairs on the back of his neck stood on end. This once innocent child was now looking at him through jet-black eyes that had white reptilian slits where the pupils should have been.

Herbert screamed as the boy smiled a shark-toothed grin at him.

The child's mouth was now full of sharp white teeth.

The old man panicked and ran the van up onto a curb and into a mailbox. It was knocked over to the sidewalk with a crash. The boy didn't move and just sat straight in the passenger seat with his head turned directly to Herbert.

The man swore as he stumbled out of the van. Trying his hardest to keep his balance.

He began to run as fast as he could down the street. He glanced back and noticed the boy was now perched on the top of his van, watching him flee. Herbert tried to run faster, but there wasn't much he could do in clown shoes and he just clip-clomped along at a hurried pace. He screamed for help, but there was no one around.

The historical district of Chillicothe was pretty desolate at night. He passed old stone storefronts and buildings that were all locked and closed. He paused every few steps to check the door handles to make sure one wasn't accidentally left open.

"Heeerrrrbeeeeeeeeerrrrrt," the boy sadistically called out as he slowly walked down the street towards the terrified old man. The clown makeup ran from his face in streaks as it mixed with sweat and tears.

"Heeerrrrbeeeeeeeeerrrrrt," the boy called out again. The demon child was in no hurry whatsoever.

The old man scrambled towards St Mary's Church. Its tall ornamental tower provided him some glimmer of hope and refuge from the nightmare child that stalked him. He ran as fast as he could while his massive clown shoes clip-clopped toward his presumed salvation.

"Heeerrrrbeeeeeeeeerrrrrt," the boy called out once more. The old clown scrambled up the stairs towards the entrance of the church. He grabbed at the handles and shook vigorously as he tried to get in. None of the doors would budge.

"Damn it! Open! I thought you fucking things were always open!" Herbert spat.

"Well, not to you, they aren't," the boy said from the bottom of the stairs. He turned around and pressed his back against the door. Herbert's screams for help fell unanswered.

"By the way. He doesn't want anything to do with you, but... I dooo," the boy said playfully.

He smiled once again to show off his rows of tiny dagger-like teeth as he pointed a finger at the stars. His black reptilian eyes burned holes into the old man's mind. Unleashing fears beyond what he had ever felt before.

It was like he was instantly taken somewhere else for a brief moment. He saw horrible images of people being tortured in horrific ways and burned alive. The sky was blood red with lakes of fire as far as he could see. He could see mountains off in the distance, with silhouettes of winged creatures flying through the air. Screams and cries for help echoed through his brain. Herbert gripped his left arm as it began to ache with pain.

"You see, I'm a big fan of your work, Herbert. Have been for some time," the boy said as he slowly climbed the stairs towards the old man. Herbert now clenched his chest as he slid down the door and faced his adversary. The boy slowly stepped up another step in his direction.

"How many children have you taken, Herbert? Love the clown angle, by the way. Who doesn't love a serial killing clown? Okay… hold on. Wait a minute, let me think," the boy paused while he put his forefinger to his temple in thought.

"I believe the count was forty-eight. Ranging from the ages of four to ten," the boy answered himself as he clapped his hands together. Herbert vomited as he still clenched his chest. His breathing became excruciatingly difficult. The boy stepped even closer.

"That's incredibly impressive. I've been following you since you started up in the early 1990s in that small shit hole town of Fargo, North Dakota. How anyone could live there is beyond me. Give me sunshine and warm weather any day. Dare I say... to hell with the cold," the six-year-old said with a giggle.

Herbert sat there staring up at the child, still holding his chest.

"Yeah, see it's been a good run buddy. Better to quit while you're still ahead, right? I mean, look at yourself. You have pretty much become a parody of who you were," the child said as he began to kneel towards Hubert. His black eyes pierced into the elderly clown's soul.

"See, the problem isn't what you have done. NO NO NO. Again, big fan here. The problem is you haven't been able to find any work for almost seven years now. So as much as I rooted for you today… It's time to go. It's time for you to move on," the child said sympathetically, as he looked over the man's painful expression with a tilt of his head.

"I've got a nice place for you all set up down there. Your kind gets the royal treatment where you are headed. I mean, we spare no expense," Milton said with a grin.

"What do you want… from me?" Herbert was barely able to get the words out as the pain in his chest became unbearable.

"Why your soul, silly. Isn't it obvious?" Milton said, with a confused expression.

Herbert's heart stopped beating, and he now lay limp in front of the church's heavy wooden doors.

"A shame it ended up this way, Herbert," Milton said as he looked down at the old man's corpse and shook his head with a sigh. He reached into his pocket and pulled out a butterscotch candy and began crinkling the wrapper as he walked off into the darkness.

As the townsfolk of Chillicothe slept safely with their families, they remained completely unaware of the cancer that had been removed from their quiet little town.

TRIGGERED

Palm trees rustled in the morning air as the sun slowly breached the horizon along the Atlantic Coast. The sky was filled with calm reds and oranges while the waves crashed against the shore. To some, this area of Florida was an eclectic wonderland of sights and sounds. Others, however, thought it was a subtropical cesspool of undesirable people.

Troy Arlington turned off the teakettle as soon as it started to whistle. Using a pot holder, he poured the steaming water into his mother's favorite coffee mug that she had used since the 1980s. The black mug had a picture of an orange cartoon cat named Garfield on it that said, "I hate Mondays." The non-offensive aroma of Earl Grey tea wafted up through the steam, opening the pores of his skin.

"Coming, Mom," he said as he turned carefully with the scalding liquid.

Troy lived with his 92-year-old mother. He moved into her house two years ago when she turned 90. Every morning now at 7 am she asked for her tea. She had been this way for as long as he could remember.

"Here you go," he said as he set the cup of tea down on the end table.

They lived in a mid-century home that looked like it was stuck in

1991. Located in New Smyrna Beach, Florida, where his mother had been a resident since the early 1980s. When Troy lost his job with NASA at the Kennedy Space Center, he moved in with her. This all happened shortly after Jan 6. 2021.

Troy sat down on a couch with a protein bar and munched on it while he checked his smartphone. His mother calmly sipped her tea and watched FOX news. He scratched at his belly through his white t-shirt.

Shut up. What the hell do you know about working? Stupid libtard. He viciously typed on one of his social media accounts. Then he scrolled through some humorous photos of people crashing on motorcycles.

LoL looks like how a liberal rides a hog, he typed. Troy continued to scroll through his phone, posting hateful comments on other people's photos.

"Did you see, Troy? Bird watching is now considered homosexual. It is now some secret code to tell if someone's a gay," she said to her son. She was sitting in a large recliner with her eyes glued to the television.

Jesus died for our country, he typed as he looked up at the TV.

"Mom, it's always been gay. I never knew anything but fruitballs to enjoy looking at stupid ole birds," Troy responded. His thumb slid upwards on his phone screen.

Just please kill yourself if you voted for Stephen Cranik. He thumbed without hesitation as he looked down from the television. With a heavy sigh, he clicked off his phone and stood up. Kissing his mother on the top of her head, he strolled towards the door.

"We'll I'm off to work Mom. If you need anything, just text me," he said while he snagged up his laptop bag and headed out the door.

Locking the door behind him, he took a deep breath of the 90% humidity that made the air feel like pea soup. The unlock button on his car keys made a chirp when he pressed it as he walked toward his Ford F-150. Tossing in his laptop case as he entered the driver's side of the truck. He got situated and pressed the start button on the dash.

"Who are we gonna get today?" he asked himself while his truck purred in response. Then he put the truck in reverse, backed out of the driveway, and headed on his way.

While driving, he ended up behind someone in a MoGo Mato EV sedan with bumper stickers that read *Vote Stephen Cranik* and one of those Grateful Dead stickers.

This made Troy's blood boil.

Look at this piece of shit. I bet he's real smug and hates white Christian men. Probably thinks we are all racists, he thought as he ground his teeth. This was the longest red light in the history of Florida.

I bet I pay my taxes so this loser can have healthcare. It's probably a Millennial who is some form of internet influencer, he continued to think as he gripped his steering wheel tighter.

The light turned green and Troy floored his truck and quickly passed the EV car in front of him and cut off the woman driving it. Unaware that she was taking her kids to a very expensive private Christian school.

He stopped at his usual Waffle House for his cup of coffee and breakfast. The restaurant smelled of old hamburger grease, bacon, and bleach water. He sat down at the counter bar and ordered his usual and waited for his cup of joe.

Scrolling through his phone, he paused at a comment left by a heavy left-wing discussion group. The picture was of a young black man that some police officers had killed senselessly. They all were brought to trial and found not guilty, allowing them to keep their jobs.

Yeah, this is a clear case of fuck around and find out. Guess the kid fucked around and found the fuck out. He typed as his coffee arrived.

"Hey Viola, how are you and Frank doing?" He asked the waitress behind the counter.

"Oh, we are okay. Having a hard time finding people to work these days. It's exhausting having to work so much," she groaned.

"Nobody wants to work anymore. They want it all for free," he said with bitterness.

A notification popped up on his phone, showing him that someone responded to his last comment. His heart raced and his mouth got dry as he picked up his phone and unlocked it.

Oh... look at you boomer... if it's not white it's not right... right boomer??? The comment read.

It instantly triggered him when he saw the "boomer" comment.

At least I work for a living. Unlike you dipshit lefties, he quickly lashed back.

Viola slid his plate across the counter. He picked up his fork and shoveled a pile of scrambled eggs into his mouth as his right thumb tapped away at his cell phone. It didn't take more than ten seconds for this phone to vibrate again to another comment notification.

Oh, tough guy... where's your white hood Mr. Grand Wizard... the response read.

This infuriated him even more. Continuing to eat his breakfast, he clicked on the user's name that was trolling him.

The account had the name Zippy Zipperson. Immediately, he thought it was a fake name. He was looking at a picture of a snowflake with a man bun holding an IPA and giving a peace sign.

Ugh, he's one of those, he thought as he started to type a response in kind.

You worthless liberals are all the same. Take take take take take. All off the backs of the working man, he said as a rebuttal.

After finishing his breakfast, he paid his check and left. Still riled up, he sped through traffic.

This is basically how every morning started for Troy. He would wake up and tend to his mother. After that, on his way to the Waffle House, someone would piss him off. Troy always found himself easily triggered when he was behind the wheel. Maybe it was because his anxiety was always intensified while he drove. Florida did have its fair share of horrible drivers.

It was 8:30 am when Troy pulled into the parking lot of the internet cafe that he had religiously gone to Monday through Friday for the past two and a half years.

Troy sat in his truck fixated on finding out more about this Zippy Zipperson. Whoever this person was, followed him on two different social media platforms he frequented. He started to wonder if it was a fake account or if it was someone he knew. Though the profile photo wasn't someone he recognized.

He shrugged it off for now and opened the driver's door to step out into the muggy Florida summer morning. He grabbed his laptop bag and locked his truck with his key fob. His phone vibrated to notify him of the activity on one of his accounts. Someone had left a comment on one of his tweets. Before taking another step, he dug his phone out of the pocket of his shorts and checked the notification.

"What in Sam Hell?" he questioned as he unlocked his phone and opened the app.

Someone had commented on something he tweeted over a year ago. His original comment was something about how all illegals should be shot out of a cannon back to their country of origin.

Oh... tough guy with a keyboard ... how's your mom??? I got something illegal for her tonight... The new comment said.

Troy became enraged when he saw it was from an account named Zippy Zipperson. He shook his head and slid his phone back into his pocket and headed into the Patriot Internet Cafe.

Troy was greeted by the internet cafe's proprietor and long-time friend Gunner Washington. He was a short stocky man with a trimmed salt-and-pepper beard. It was believed that Gunner was a Desert Storm veteran and served with the Marines. He never spoke about it to anyone but clearly, he enjoyed the mystery that surrounded him.

"Morning, Troy," the man said as his rottweiler padded over to greet him with excitement.

"Hey, Gunner. Hey Booth," he responded as he bent down to pat the big lummox on his head. Booth snorted and wagged his stub of a tail.

"You know you're the only one he does that with," Gunner said as his dog trotted back past him and flopped down on his bed.

"That's just cuz I've eaten so much beef jerky in my life. I think I permanently smell like the stuff," Troy said and shrugged his shoulders.

The Patriot Internet Cafe was opened in early 2019. Gunner created a cybercafe where like-minded people could come and work or just surf the internet without being judged. The 1200-square-foot cafe had a long table that ran down the center of the room. There were workstations set up on either side totaling 10 in all. Along the back wall facing the storefront were individual desktop computers that were open for public use. Gunner charged $10 an hour to use his cafe and always supplied free coffee and bagels if you got there early enough. He only had two rules; no porn and don't hack the CIA.

"Mike and Steve coming today?" Troy asked after he placed his laptop bag on the center table.

"I haven't seen or heard from Steve in a while. He hasn't been online either. Mike should be here in a few minutes," Gunner said. The man walked back into his office with a bagel in his mouth and a fresh cup of coffee in his hand.

That's odd, Troy thought to himself, pulling his laptop out.

Steve's been coming here every day since Gunner opened the cafe.

I hope he's okay. Troy thought as he felt some concern for Steve, but it was short-lived due to his own need for a social media fix.

Troy had been coming to Gunner's cafe ever since he lost his job at the Kennedy Space Center. He had worked at the KSC for 15 years before being fired. He was one of the leading aerospace engineers that specialized in propulsion and combustion. When the news coverage of what happened at the US Capitol on January 6th, 2021, hit the airwaves, the proverbial shit hit the fan. On national television, Troy was shown marching up the steps of the Capitol building. Once the higher-ups at NASA saw him on the news, he was quickly and not quietly, terminated.

When he met his wife Megan in 2002, things were way different. Troy was a very soft-spoken creative who usually leaned much more liberal than he was today. He always loved his conspiracy theories, but just treated them as entertainment. He married Megan four years after they met. At first, it was bliss. They had two wonderful daughters by the name of Willow and Hope.

It wasn't until the development of smartphones and social media that his demeanor started to change. His wife of 13 years left him in the summer of 2019. With the growth of social media and the creation of algorithms, Troy began to devour all types of conspiracy theories. The more he discovered, the more his smartphone showed him. It became an addiction that would cost him more than his marriage and his job. Nowadays, he came to Gunner's Patriot Cafe to feed his addiction like a compulsive gambler at a horse track.

Troy's mother was very sharp for 92 years old but still never put two and two together that he no longer worked for NASA. She never realized that 90% of the time when he was leaving for work, Troy wore a t-shirt, and shorts with flip-flops.

"What up losers!" Mike bellowed as he entered the cafe. They both noticed his t-shirt read "Black Rifles Matter".

"Dude, nice shirt," Gunner said.

Booth just laid on his bed and watched Mike enter the cafe.

"Yeah, I ordered it online a while back. Just something to add to my collection to make them snowflakes squirm," he said proudly.

Mike was known for wearing shirts that more or less pushed the PC envelope. He didn't care one way or another. To him, if you didn't like it, too bad.

"So what did the kid at Starbucks say when you walked in wearing that?" Troy asked while he pointed at the cup in Mike's hand.

"Was pale as a ghost, but the customers are always right... Right?" Mike answered with a laugh.

"Ha! Yeah," Troy responded.

"Have you heard from Steve?" Gunner asked while he gave Mike a cheese bagel.

"Thanks... No, I haven't. Last I heard, he had found out something and was going to check it out," Mike said as he took a bite of bagel. Eating half of it in one chomp. He wasn't a skinny man by any stretch and at six foot four, he could really pack away the carbs.

"Check something out? Check what out?" Troy asked in confusion.

"Don't know. That was all he said, and that was over a week ago," Mike replied. He set a laptop case on the center table across from Troy. Unzipped the bag and pulled his laptop out onto the table.

"Shall we get started?" Gunner asked.

The three of them got together Monday through Friday for eight hours a day only to troll the internet. Their primary goal was to help take their country back.

The three provocateurs always started with trolling certain news websites. Attacking what they would call the liberal media. To them, the scourge of the country. Once they moved through the news platforms, they made their way over to their social media platforms. They all had a couple of fake accounts they logged into in case they got blocked or reported.

Gunner was a computer whiz and considered himself a decent hacker. He had multiple ways to get around things so they could keep up their fight against socialism.

Troy was typing away in a triggered discussion on one of the news platforms based in New York City. Suddenly his phone exploded with alerts.

"What the holy fuck?" he spat. His phone told him he had 37 notifications.

"Dude, is that your phone going off?" Mike asked as he leaned over from behind his laptop.

"Yeah!" Troy said with frustration.

He cleared his notifications and quickly logged off the New York Times website. When he pulled up one of his social media profiles, he noticed 17 comments on various posts he had made throughout the week. His heart began to race as blood shot through his veins.

Oh… look at the boomer… he knows how to use a computer… probably took him a week to learn how to turn it on… One comment read.

How's your mom??? Another one read. Troy got more frustrated and obsessed the more he read.

Did it take you two hours to figure out how to type this comment??? The next one read.

Hey Troy... how do boomers change a light bulb??? They don't... they just stand around and complain about how much better the old ones were... Another comment read, followed by what looked like eggplant emojis.

All the comments were made with the same profile: Zippy Zipperson. Whoever was behind this profile was beginning to piss him off. Mike noticed his keystrokes were becoming louder and heavier.

"You okay over there, hoss?" Mike asked Troy, who was red-faced and flustered.

"I'm pissed off, Mike," he replied as he continued to read the next comment on another platform.

Why do boomers always pay by check... Troy??? They hate change... This comment was followed by three skull and crossbones emojis. Those three simple pixel shapes that were programmed to look like an 8-bit skull and crossbones triggered Troy into a crimson haze. Steam practically squirted from his ears.

"Some fucktard named Zippy Zipperson has been trolling me all morning!" Troy spat.

Mike leaned over from behind his computer screen.

"What name did you say?" He asked with a raised eyebrow.

"Zipper motherfucking Zipperson and I think he just sent me a threat," he responded.

He read him the last comment out loud and described the three emojis.

"That, to me, is a threat. Whoever the fuck this is just told me he's gonna come for me," Troy said convincingly.

"You know what, I think that's the name Steve mentioned a week ago," Mike said and rubbed his chin in thought.

"Argh! Here's another one," Troy belted and read the comment out loud.

"Says the 56-year-old loser that lives with his mom. Ok boomer," Troy said.

"Yup, see here," Mike said as he pointed at his screen. Troy got up and walked around the table. At the same time, Gunner came out of his office.

"I pulled up a couple of Steve's last posts and a couple of his different profiles," Mike said.

He pointed out the comment sections of some of Steve's posts. The other two leaned in to look closer.

"Right here. See, someone with a profile Zippy Zipperson had commented on his last couple of posts," Mike pointed.

"See there," Troy pointed out a comment that had three skulls and crossbones emojis. The other two reflexively nodded.

"And now, he's MIA," Gunner said, then crossed his arms.

"Here. You can see that this guy likes to use punctuation in threes," Mike said and pointed to three periods after every pause in a sentence.

"Have you responded yet?" Gunner asked.

"No, I'm still reading," Troy responded.

"Don't yet," Gunner said.

"Yeah, he's right. Let's find out whatever we can about this Zippy Zipperhead or whatever the fuck his name is," Mike said.

"Yeah, that sounds good. Let's stalk our prey," Troy responded through squinted eyes. Then he walked back over to his computer.

Gunner went over and filled up a coffee mug.

"You know I can probably find his IP address and then pinpoint the location," Gunner said in a conspiratorial tone and shrugged.

"Dude… how rad would it be if we found this fucker and knocked on his front door?" Mike asked while rubbing his palms together.

"Holy fuck, that would rule. Talk about 'hashtag' woke," Troy responded, and they all laughed.

They all went back to work at their computers, trying to find out everything they could about Zippy Zipperson.

"See, right here he's posting reviews for restaurants I go to," Troy said. He scrolled through some reviews and noticed they were all directed towards him.

What do you call a 56-year-old in a jet??? A Sonic Boomer... One review comment read.

This was personal to him now. He wondered if Steve had found something out about Zippy and he ended up being kidnapped or worse. Troy had known Steve since 2020. They had both been in DC on January 6th. He chuckled for a minute at the thought of some pansy-ass hipster millennial trying to take Steve down.

"Got it!" Gunner called out from his office. Booth raised his head at the sound of his owner's voice, then laid back down with a sense of annoyance. "Got the IP address," Gunner called out.

"Oh yeah? That was fast," Mike said, looking at Troy.

"Yeah, it was pretty easy to get. Now all I need to do is see if I can find where it's coming from," he said while he bobbed his head up and down to himself.

"Let me know what you find," Troy said as he looked through photos of Zippy Zipperson.

All the photos matched each other. None of them seemed like they were of a different person. Whoever created these profiles went to a lot of work to make them all match. He still didn't know how he felt about whether Zippy was a real person. This was a lot of work for someone who was just out trolling people on a fake account. Troy was beginning to believe this Zippy Zipperson was real.

"Man, if Gunner finds this douchebag, we have to pay him a visit. I would love to see some woke-ass millennial piss their pants at the sight of us," Mike said with a huge smile.

"Yeah, can you imagine? We could even sic ole Booth on him," Troy said while he looked down at the snoring 145-pound side of beef.

"Why the heck did he name his dog Booth?" Mike asked as the dog opened his eyes at the sound of his name.

"Because that's the name of the man that shot the guy that freed the slaves. Cuz everything basically went downhill after that," Troy said as he chuckled.

Mike nodded and acknowledged what he just heard.

"KIGY," Mike said.

"AKIA," Troy responded without hesitation.

They both nodded and went back to looking at their screen.

Troy was not or never had been in the Klan. He did, however, fantasize about it. He also had a good understanding of the acronyms they used to secretly communicate. In the end, he knew he was too much of a wimp to ever become a full member.

They all worked at this until it was dark outside. Nobody else came into the Patriot Internet Cafe at all that day. That was pretty typical these days. Gunner always said it was because everyone was too paranoid now. He felt that the government was starting to come down on cyber security and no one wanted to risk getting busted.

Sadly, that wasn't why the cafe was always empty. Gunner had a very loud mouth on him and the community did not care much for him. He was extremely abrasive and standoffish. If you didn't agree with Gunner, then you were the enemy. He was all ride or die.

"Shit, I gotta get back. Mom needs her dinner," Troy said and quickly closed his laptop.

"Yeah, I need to get home, too. Not that I want to because all my wife is gonna do it bitch at me when I get home," Mike said as he shut down his computer.

"I'm gonna stay a bit longer," Gunner said after cracking open a beer.

Booth just groaned and rolled over.

Gunner walked over to the two men and offered them both a cold beer.

"I think I can have this guy's address and social security number by morning. Also, I hit up my buddy over at the precinct and he's gonna run this guy's record," Gunner said with a sneer.

"Everything?" Mike asked, then slammed back his can of beer in three loud gulps and belched.

"Yup," Gunner said proudly.

Booth groaned again like he was growing increasingly annoyed at the amount of talking that was going on.

"Outstanding man. I'm gonna take my beer with me. I'll drink it on the way home. Gotta take care of mom," he said. Troy then snatched up his laptop bag and made his way to the door.

"Blur und Ehre," Mike replied in German.

Hey Mom," Troy said as he entered the house. His mother was in the same chair she was in when he left this morning. The television was still on the same station.

"Troy? Is that you?" she asked.

"Yeah Mom, sorry I had to work so late. Been working on a new propulsion system for the Space X program," he replied. "Let me help you to the bathroom."

After he helped his mother back from the bathroom, he made sure she was comfortable. Troy walked to the kitchen and opened a beer with a moan, and took a huge drink. He checked his phone and saw that there were more notifications.

"Jesus Christ, does this guy ever let up?" he said to himself as he scrolled through multiple comments.

Troy was having a very hard time having someone do to him what he had done to so many others. He had no idea how many people he hurt in the past. This obsession he developed had cost him his marriage, his relationship with his children, and his job. Troy didn't see it that way, though. He felt that he was a crusader for good and he understood the costs and sacrifices that needed to be made.

While placing a frozen dinner in the microwave for his mother, he began to wonder about Steve. As he watched the dinner go in circles through its little window, he began to mutter to himself.

"What the hell had Steve uncovered?" He took a pull off his beer bottle.

His mind went into high gear. Did he find out who this Zippy Zipperhead was? Steve wasn't the type of guy to be pushed around. Troy saw him break some dude's jaw once with one punch. Steve was not the kinda man someone fucked with. The microwave beeped three times, bringing him back to the moment at hand. He then placed the frozen dinner on a TV tray and opened a diet soda from the fridge.

"Food's ready, mom," he said, then walked into the living room with the tray.

"Oh thank you, honey," she said as he placed the tray in her lap.

"Your favorite, Orange Chicken," Troy said, then he plopped on the couch next to her.

"I used to get my hair done by an oriental woman. That was years ago. She had these tiny little hands and did great work. Barely spoke English though," she said while she crammed a spoonful of Orange Chicken into her mouth. Troy was too distracted by his phone to listen. A notification popped up from his Messenger app. His heart began to race as he noticed it was from Steve.

Troy... you gotta help me... I'm trapped under the Turnbull Ruins... the message read.

He blankly stared at his phone, not hearing a word his mother was saying. He quickly fired off a group text to Gunner and Mike.

Guys, you won't believe this, but I just heard from Steve. I think.? His message to the group read.

Yeah, me too, Mike quickly responded.

Same. I've also found out a lot about Mr. Zipperhead, Gunner replied.

Oh yeah? Troy texted back.

Yes, let's meet up at the cafe tomorrow morning at 8 am and come up with a game plan. In the meantime, do NOT respond to either Steve or Zipperhead, Gunner's text instructed.

"Hell yeah!" Troy shouted out loud and scared his mother in the process.

"Jesus H Christ, Troy! Watch your language and bring me another Diet Coke," his mother demanded. Troy bowed his head and walked into the kitchen.

10-4, Mike responded in return.

Troy paused a minute to think about the message he got from who he thought was Steve. Why did he use Messenger? Also, why didn't he call or text like normal? Was he hacked? Was this really Steve? All of these thoughts raced through his head. He opened the fridge door and grabbed a Diet Coke. Then his phone vibrated.

Another message from Steve came through.

Troy, you have to help me... please... I'm hurt bad... The message said.

He just stared at his phone, not knowing what to do. Gunner told him not to respond and assumed he wanted everyone to have radio silence until they met up in the morning. He just continued to stand in the kitchen and look at his phone. He shook his head to bring him back to reality and then turned to leave the kitchen and bring his mother her Diet Coke. Before he made it out of the kitchen, his phone went off once more. It was a text message from an unknown number.

Sup... Boomer... The message read.

Troy dropped the can of diet soda. His heart started to race, and he swore out loud.

"Language!" his mother shouted from the living room.

Troy grumbled and started to clean up the spilled soft drink. His phone dinged again.

How's your mom... Troy... The next message read.

His face flushed red, and his hands began to shake. His phone dinged again.

She sure likes to watch TV... the text read.

Troy froze. He quickly stormed past his mother and opened the front door. The warm ocean breeze blew through the living room. He continued out onto the front porch. His eyes darted from side to side as he searched for anything out of place. He heard his mother call out behind him. He ignored her voice and focused on his surroundings. The palm trees rustled in the wind and there was a faint sound of a dog barking in the distance.

They were only one street west of A1A which ran along the Atlantic Coast. Other than the occasional car driving by, there was nothing out of the ordinary. Against his better judgment, he replied to the text message. He typed a triggered response, then deleted it. Then he repeated the process a few more times until he stopped and took a deep breath.

His anger and impatience were getting the best of him. Trying to calm himself, he walked back into the house. Still ignoring his mother as she tried to ask what was going on.

"What's going on Troy?" She asked, exasperated.

He just waved his hand at her as he stormed past. Walking into the kitchen, he snatched up another bottle of beer from the fridge, opened it, and took a drink.

Who is this? He finally responded.

Within seconds, he could see the little dots blinking, indicating someone was responding. He nervously took a screenshot of the text message chain while he waited. He didn't want something to happen, and not have any evidence.

Why it's Zippy... You're a hard man to find... The response said.

Troy's face went pale.

The boys met up at the Patriot Internet Cafe at 8 am as planned. Troy was the first one there and was waiting in his truck, scrolling through photos of whoever this Zippy Zipperson was. Mike and Gunner pulled up about the same time. Mike had on a t-shirt that said "I stand for the flag and kneel for the cross."

"Nice shirt," Troy said as he got out of his truck.

Gunner unlocked the front door as Booth pushed his way past him, went to his bed, and flopped down with a grunt.

"Does that dog do anything else but bum around? Shit, he's like my ex-wife," Mike said with a laugh.

Gunner shrugged as his dog groaned and rolled over, facing away from them.

"Oh, he's a badass. Don't let him fool you. I just gotta give the right command and he goes into beast mode," Gunner said.

Booth began to snore. Gunner turned on the lights while the other two placed their laptop bags on the center table.

"Okay, so this fucker got my phone number somehow. He texted me a few times last night after we got the messages from Steve," Troy said, then pulled out his computer.

Gunner furrowed his brow. "I don't think that was Steve messaging us last night. Did you notice the punctuation he or she was using?" he noted as he brewed a pot of coffee.

"Yeah, I thought that too," Mike said while he powered up his laptop.

Troy logged into his messenger app and pulled up Steve's last message.

"Did you guys get a second message from Steve, or I mean Not Steve?" Troy said as he pointed to his computer screen.

Gunner raised his eyebrow and walked over to look.

"No? Did you Gunner?" Mike responded.

Gunner shook his head as he bent over to read the message that Troy was pointing to.

"Hmmm. This is very interesting. Whoever this is definitely has a hard-on for you, Troy," Gunner said.

"You pissed anyone off lately?" Mike asked.

Troy just laughed. "Daily," he responded.

The other two chuckled at his response. Gunner poured a cup of coffee.

"I was able to find his IP geolocation. See, by mapping his IP address to the specific geographic location of the internet he has been using. Whatever device these messages have been coming from, I found it. I've been able to find his country, zip code, longitude and latitude, ISP, area code, and basically wherever he takes a shit," Gunner said proudly.

Taking another sip of coffee, he continued while the other two looked at him with blank faces.

"I also heard back from my Private Eye friend who pulled up everything attached to this account and name. Of course, Zippy Zipperson is not a real name. By comparing public records with the locations of his IP address, nothing whatsoever came up. I mean nothing. This dude's a ghost. This is spook-level hacker shit," Gunner said as he rummaged through a box of stale bagels.

"And?" Troy asked.

Mike looked back and forth between the two of them. Booth sensed the tension and padded over and put his chin on Troy's thigh.

"Dude might be a ghost, but I found exactly where he is," Gunner said. He tore apart an onion bagel with determination.

"Well, where is he?" Mike asked impatiently. Gunner seemed to be relishing this conversation with pride.

"Turnbull Ruins," he responded.

Both Mike and Troy looked at each other.

"So exactly what Steve's message said?" Mike asked.

"Yup. Whoever this is, is baiting us. I think Steve found out something and went to check it out. He's tough as shit, so if he went down, it wasn't easy," Gunner said. Tearing off another piece of bagel and stuffing it in his mouth.

"Okay, okay, hold on," Troy interjected and pet Booth on the head.

Mike leaned over from behind his computer screen.

"Okay, so why would whoever this internet troll is tell us exactly where they are? That doesn't make any sense," Troy rebutted.

Gunner raised an eyebrow.

"I mean, think about it. The entire point of trolling people on the internet is that people don't know where or who you are," Troy said as he scratched the dog behind his left ear.

"Yeah. I think Troy has a point. Why the hell would someone do that? Unless it was really Steve," Mike added.

Gunner paused, thinking about what to say next.

"I've got a plan. I say we go check out the Trumbull Ruins tonight. We either fuck some shit up or we find and help Steve," Gunner responded, taking a long sip from his coffee.

"I like that plan. Sounds like a win-win. Clearly whoever this is, is some liberal who doesn't know who they just messed with," Mike replied as he slammed his fist down on the table.

Gunner nodded in response.

"Okay, okay, I guess you guys are right. I mean, we either scare the shit outta this person or we find Steve," Troy reluctantly agreed.

The other two gave each other a malicious smirk.

"I think someone just fucked around and is about to find out," Gunner said sternly.

Booth chuffed and padded over to his bed and flopped down.

"I think your dog just rolled his eyes at you," Troy said.

"So what's the plan, Gunner?" Mike asked, then closed his laptop.

Gunner smiled. Troy nervously listened. Going after people on the internet was one thing, but going after people was another thing altogether.

"Whelp, how I figure it is we are either Steve's extraction team or a can of whoop ass for whoever has been doing this," Gunner said.

Troy looked at Mike for a response.

"Hell yeah!" Mike responded.

Troy was starting to wonder if this was going too far. Maybe they should call the cops and file a missing person report for Steve. He could just block the accounts trolling him and block the phone number. Would that make him a chickenshit? No, whoever this was wasn't going to stop. They had to be dealt with.

"Go on," Troy added.

"My plan is to go in hot. Expect a target-rich environment. Mike and I will do a little recon first. Troy, I want you to reply to everything and keep replying. Really play into this," Gunner said as he paced back and forth.

"Yeah, I like that idea. You and I can check things out while it's daylight. You planning on us going back once it's dark?" Mike asked.

"Yup. Troy, you can stay here and use my office and hang with Booth. Mike and I will go check things out. After that we will close up shop and meet back here at 2200 hours," Gunner said.

Booth raised his head at the sound of his voice. Realizing there were no treats involved, he sighed and laid his head back down.

"It's about 8:30 am right now. I say we get started," Mike interjected.

"You packing?" Gunner asked.

"Always. Never know what's gonna happen," Mike responded.

Troy still had mixed feelings, but figured he'd go along for the ride and see where this went.

"Alright, I'll start trolling Mr. Zipperhead. Then lock up when I leave," he responded.

Troy showed back up at the Patriot Cafe around 10 pm. Mike and Gunner were already there. Both of them were decked out in full tactical gear. Mike looked a little silly because it didn't exactly fit his body type. He looked like 280 pounds of sausage meat packed into 20 pounds of casing. He was about to burst at the seams. Even Booth had a tactical dog vest on. Troy wasn't exactly sure why, and by the look on the dog's face, he didn't either.

They all stood in Gunner's back office looking at the arsenal laid out on his desk in front of them. Troy quickly realized he was underdressed in his cargo shorts, Hawaiian shirt, and sneakers.

Mike was clearing and reloading a Springfield 1911 .45 caliber handgun while Gunner was loading rounds into a magazine for his rifle. His prized possession was a Sig Sauer SIG516 AR-15 style rifle. He quickly thumbed the 5.56 nato round into the metal clip.

"Isn't this a bit much?" Troy asked nervously. Being the only one to not own a firearm, he was feeling a little out of place.

"Nope," Gunner said as he snapped another bullet in place.

Mike slid his pistol into his holster on his hip and handed Troy an extra vest.

"Here, this should fit. Put it on. I've also got a spare Glock 19 you can carry," Mike said.

Booth pressed his head into the side of Troy's right leg and looked up at him with a look of concern. Almost like he was telling Troy this was not a good idea.

"Okay," Troy said as he slipped on the vest and tightened the straps.

Gunner slapped his clip into his rifle but didn't cock it. Mike handed out a couple of sets of zip-tie cuffs. They all slipped them under the webbing of their vests. Troy dropped the Glock into the front pocket of his shorts. The weight was causing them to feel like they were going to fall. He knew he looked ridiculous, but he didn't want to take any shit from the other two, so he just played along.

"Okay, so here's the plan," Gunner said after he slid his Kabar knife into its sheath on his right breast.

Mike also had a fixed-blade knife on his belt. Troy looked at Booth and the dog tilted his head in confusion.

"Mike and I found a hatch at the ruins. The surrounding ground was trampled pretty good. I'm almost positive they are using that to go in and out of whatever they have going on down there," Gunner stated while sliding another magazine into a pouch on his left breast.

"Wait? Did you say 'They'?" Troy interrupted.

Mike nodded back. "Yeah, we think this has to be a multi-person operation. Probably cooking meth down there too," he said.

"As I was saying. The hatch looks like it can be easily opened with a crowbar. I'll go first with Booth, then you two follow," Gunner continued.

"What if it's like a manhole with a ladder? How does Booth get down?" Troy asked and pointed at the dog.

"I've got some carabiners and rope. We will lower him down if we have to. Regardless, once we are in, we'll move fast. Look for any signs of life. Then head that way," Gunner said.

"So we have no idea what's down there and we have no idea what condition it's in?" Troy said inquisitively. He could sense the other two were beginning to get frustrated with him. He just couldn't shake the fact that this was the dumbest thing he's ever attempted.

"Yeah. Ain't it cool?" Mike asked with a grin.

"The idea is to not shoot anyone. Scare em. Then maybe smack 'em around. Slap on some zip-ties and make sure they know who we are and this is what happens when you fuck around and find out," Gunner stated sternly.

"Who exactly are we?" Troy asked in puzzlement.

Booth sat down next to him with a grunt like he was also waiting for the answer as well.

"Patriots. We stand for the flag and kneel for the cross," Gunner said. Proudly giving a salute to the American flag in the corner of his office.

"Damn straight," Mike said while he saluted in return.

Troy furrowed his brow and just looked down at Booth, who simultaneously looked up at him.

"Okay, then what?" Troy asked but knew they would be annoyed.

"We beat the shit out of them," Mike said with a laugh.

Troy noticed there was a half empty fifth of Jim Beam on Gunner's desk.

"Fuck it," Troy spat as he snatched up the Jim Beam.

The four of them climbed into Gunner's black Ford F-250 dually pickup. Troy made sure his shorts didn't fall down as he stepped up into the truck. Booth sat next to him behind Mike in the passenger seat.

"There's three big Maglites behind your seat, Troy, with fresh batteries," Gunner said as he looked in his rear-view mirror. Troy nodded back.

Gunner fired up his power stroke diesel and off they went to the Turnbull Ruins.

"Is it bad to be turned on right now?" Mike asked.

Both Troy and Gunner raised an eyebrow at each other through the rearview mirror.

The hatch they were looking for was a four-by-five rectangle located on the south side of the ruins. They easily got it open and quietly laid it down on the ground. To all of their surprise, it was a stone staircase. Gunner slid his Maglite into a holster on his thigh. Taking his Sig Sauer off his right shoulder, he switched on the barrel-mounted light.

"Booth! Seek!" Gunner spat in a whisper.

On any given day that command would have meant something to the rottweiler, but today wasn't one of them. Booth just planted his butt firmly on the ground and looked at his owner.

"Booth! Seek!" he repeated.

This time, he whispered louder.

Booth continued to just stare at Gunner. Mike snickered. Troy sensed the dog knew something they didn't. This didn't seem to settle his nerves.

"You useless shithead," Gunner grumbled as he started his descent down the stone staircase.

Mike followed, and then Troy followed Mike. Booth finally trailed after Troy.

Right away, Gunner noticed an electrical conduit ruining down the wall up near the ceiling.

"I'm guessing that's a recent addition," he said as he shined the light at it.

"Bet there's a fiber-optic cable in there," Mike pointed out.

They continued down the staircase for another 50 ft, before reaching the bottom. Once on the ground, they could sense this place had been here a very long time. In front of them was a long hallway made out of similar stone as the ruins above. The air was cool and humid. The smell of musty mold and mildew mixed with something very old. They couldn't place it. Was it natural gas or something else?

"What the fuck is this place, man?" Mike whispered as he shined his flashlight all around him.

"I think this is as old as the ruins up top. I'm guessing at some point in the last couple of decades, someone placed a hatch over the entrance," Troy said. He leaned forward and studied the wall. It was damp and cool to the touch.

About 25 steps down the tunnel, Troy noticed some primitive drawings on one part of the wall. The picture depicted a group of what looked like bipedal humanoids. They were of all different body types, but their limbs all seemed elongated. The primitive drawings showed them having long claws and sharp teeth.

"Umm, guys?" Troy asked as Mike and Gunner continued cautiously down the corridor. Troy noticed that they didn't hear him and he didn't want to raise his voice.

Booth was keeping his distance behind everyone. This worried Troy… A lot.

"What do you sense, boy?" Troy said as he bent down.

The dog would not come any closer.

"Psst, we gotta move," Mike quietly called down the corridor.

Troy stopped what he was doing and began to catch up. Booth still slowly crept along, warily watching his step.

"Guys, did you see those drawings on the wall back there? They looked pretty old and were of some kind of creature," Troy whispered while pointing his thumb over his shoulder.

Gunner placed his finger over his lips to hush Troy as he pointed down the dark corridor. The path in front of them forked in two directions.

"Shit, which way do we go?" Mike whispered.

They both waited for Gunner to respond. Troy took a minute and tried to listen to their surroundings. There was a faint hum coming from the left corridor.

Gunner pointed up at the conduit running along the wall that went left. He placed his hand on Mike's shoulder and pointed down the other corridor. This instructed Mike to go in that direction. Then Gunner signaled at Troy and directed him to follow along to the left.

Mike nodded and unholstered his .45. He shined his Maglite in front of him and held his pistol down at his side. As Gunner and Troy went left and Mike went right, Booth watched them all before deciding to sulk slowly after Mike.

As Mike walked down the corridor, he noticed a candy wrapper on the ground in front of him. He knelt down and set his pistol on the stone floor. Reaching down, he snatched up the wrapper and examined it in the light of his flashlight.

"Snickers?" he whispered as he examined the crumpled-up wrapper. He sniffed it and noticed it had a rotten egg smell.

Booth crept up next to him with a worried look.

"Hey boy, you smell that too?" He whispered.

Booth responded with a quiet whine.

Mike shined his flashlight down the length of the tunnel and saw two more wrappers ahead of them. They both moved forward as the hair on their necks stood up a bit.

Meanwhile, down the left corridor, Troy and Gunner continued to follow the metal conduit down the ancient hallway. Neither of them spoke. Troy was focused on making sure nothing was behind them. They both looked at each other when they noticed the humming sound had slowly gotten louder.

"I think we are getting closer," Gunner carefully whispered to Troy.

Troy nodded in return. Deep down, he regretted his decision to do this more and more with every step. There was also a foul odor creeping towards them the deeper they went.

"Smell that?" Troy whispered.

Gunner nodded. He brought his Sig Sauer up against his shoulder and carefully continued forward. His barrel-mounted light illuminated their path through the depths of the ancient ruins. Troy placed his hand on the wall to his right and noticed it was damp and much colder than it was from where they first entered.

Mike and Booth now saw that the corridor opened up into what looked like a room about 30 feet in front of them. There was now an overpowering smell of something horrible mixed with a sulphuric smell.

Booth whimpered as they continued.

The hallway ended in a stone archway that opened up into a room filled with what looked like a large pile of garbage. It appeared to be a collection of discarded candy wrappers, potato chip bags, and empty cans of Mountain Dew. The smell was so bad Mike placed the back of his forearm up against his mouth and nose. Booth did not cross the threshold into the room as the large man entered. The dog just stood there with his head low, keeping a watchful eye as Mike examined the room.

When Mike got a closer look, he saw that it was mostly empty wrappers and old soda cans littered about in front of him. After a few moments, he noticed that there were human bones scattered among the garbage. Some of them appeared to be fresher than others. He could feel his size 12 combat boots stick to the ground as he slowly walked closer to the pile. It reminded him of the cheap, one-dollar movie theaters he went to as a child. Upon getting a closer look, he recognized what appeared to be human remains poking through the rubbish.

Next to an empty two-liter bottle of Code Red Mountain Dew was a severed arm. It appeared to be fresh and looked like it had been gnawed on by an alligator. At a closer look, he saw a tattoo of a Confederate flag on the upper bicep. The words written underneath that said, "Don't Tread On Me."

"Jesus Christ! It's Steve!" Mike spat and quickly turned away.

This was too much for him to take between the smell, and seeing his missing friend's severed arm, he tried to cover his mouth and turn away. When the contents of his stomach decided to stay where they were, he turned to notice that Booth was wagging his stump of a tail.

He was severely confused as to why the dog seemed so excited. The dog snorted and shook its butt as it wagged its tail. Every three or four shakes of his rump, Booth would spin in a circle. It was as if he was waiting for a treat or greeting his master after he returned home from a long trip.

"What the hell are you doing, dumbass?" Mike questioned the big furry lummox as it entered a play posture.

A sudden rustling noise behind him made his heart stop. There was a wheezing noise that sounded like some prepubescent teenager with asthma was standing right behind him. Mike could feel something's warm breath on the back of his neck. He instantly reached for his pistol and realized it wasn't there. It was still back down the hallway where he last left it.

A large hand landed on top of his shaved head and slowly spun him around. The overweight man began to cry when he saw what was behind him. Something shaped like a very tall man stepped out of the shadows. At first, Mike thought it was smiling at him until it began to open its mouth to an impossible gape. Rows of yellowed, jagged teeth seem to protrude from the creature's black gums. The smell of halitosis and sulfur burned his nostrils as its gaping maw widened even more. Mike stood frozen as tears ran down his cheeks.

Booth just continued to wag his tail and spin in circles with excitement. He was doing the best he could to contain himself. He was waiting for his new friend to finish whatever he was doing with his old friend. Shadows danced in the reflection of the dog's eyes as his old friend was relieved of his appendages.

Mike finally fell silent. A clawed hand with long bony fingers slowly reached towards the rottweiler. Booth couldn't hold in his excitement. The dog's rear end began to hop up and down as it wagged its tail. The hand was still dripping with Mike's blood and viscera. Its long black talons protruded from each finger. Booth spun in a circle once more and snorted.

"Puuupppy... good," the creature said in broken English as it patted the dog gently on top of his head.

Gunner and Troy continued down their corridor and were beginning to realize this was more of a labyrinth than just a simple tunnel system. Troy noticed more ancient drawings along the stone walls depicting the same humanoid creatures. He tried to point them out to Gunner, but he was too hyper-focused on where they were going to even care.

They followed the conduit on the wall through the maze of tunnels that seemed to go on for miles. Troy could tell they were still at the same level and had not gone any deeper underground. If he had to guess, he would say that they had gone at least two miles from where they entered the hatch. Troy was grateful that all they had to do was follow the conduit back the way they came to find their way out. Gunner held up his right fist to signal them both to a halt. Neither of them said a word.

Gunner aimed his light down the corridor in front of them and pointed toward an archway off to the left. What caught their attention was the jumble of cables that came out from the doorway and down the hallway in front of them. They could now hear the sound of the hum they had been following. Gunner reached into his pants pocket as he held his rifle aimed down the hallway. He retrieved his cell phone and was not surprised to see he did not have a signal. With a swipe of his thumb, Gunner unlocked his phone screen and opened up his notepad. He quickly typed something and then showed it to Troy.

I think this is where their power supply is. I bet we find a generator just inside that doorway. The conduit must just be fiber wire for their internet, the note read.

Troy gave an understanding nod. His palms were beginning to sweat and his nerves were on edge. This was happening. He gave serious thought to just turning around and leaving Gunner down here and going home. This was all too crazy for him. In the time they had been down here, he had lots of opportunities to think about his life.

He began to wonder where it all went wrong. Just a little over five years ago, he was working for NASA, making great money, and had a wife and kids who loved him. All because he was obsessed with the news, politics, and conspiracy theories, his life changed. It dawned on him he was no longer the man he once was.

They came to the doorway, and Gunner shined his light inside the small circular room. He was correct. There was a quiet 24kw generator humming away in the room, supplying power to God knows what further down the maze. Troy pulled out his cell phone opened it to his notepad, and began typing with his thumbs.

Should we turn it off? Like, kill the power? His note read.

Gunner's brow furrowed as he began to do the same on his cellphone in response.

No, we still have the element of surprise. We don't want these fuckers knowing what's coming for them. His response read.

Troy's stomach dropped at the thought of violence. It was one thing to talk about it, but an entirely different thing to seek it out and go through with it.

They walked back out into the corridor and Troy thought he heard something from back the way they came. He quickly shined his Maglite back down the hallway and caught a glimpse of a set of eyes reflecting back at him in the darkness. Then quickly they were gone, like nothing was even there.

"Did you see that?" he whispered to Gunner.

"No," Gunner whispered back and shook his head.

He motioned for them to continue walking and following the conduit. Now they also had the power cables along the ground to follow. They walked another 50 feet and the maze once again branched off into two separate tunnels. The conduit went down the path to the right, where they could see a small hint of light flickering in the shadows. The path to the left just went into darkness. There was that strange rotten-egg scent that was now mixing with the damp mildew of the corridor.

"What's that smell?" Troy whispered.

Gunner held his finger to his lips and turned off his tactical light.

Troy quickly clicked off his Maglite as well. Now they stood there in the darkness with the faint glow down the right chamber being the only source of light. There was a squeaking noise from the opposite corridor. It almost sounded like a dog toy.

"Booth?" Gunner whispered.

They could barely see anything even after their vision adapted.

"Booth, is that you boy?" he repeated.

The squeaking got louder and faster.

"So much for the element of surprise," Troy whispered.

They heard the dog snort and his nails click and clack on the stone floor. He pranced up to them, squeaking a chew toy excitedly. Gunner hesitated a moment, then switched on his light to get a better look at what was going on.

Troy was unable to move paralyzed with fright while Gunner stood fixated on his dog, spinning in excitement in front of him.

Just inside the archway of the left corridor stood a tall creature of disproportionate features. It had to be at least seven feet tall and seemed to duck under the archway. The monster had a barrel chest and a skinny midsection, with gangly arms and long legs that seemed too long for its body. Its sinewy fingers ended in black talons and clicked together with anticipation. A hook-like nose separated two beady, milky-yellow eyes. Pointed ears jetted out from either side of its bald head as its mouth opened and closed, causing rows of sharp teeth to chatter. Troy instantly recognized it from the primitive drawings on the stone walls they passed earlier. The first thing that popped into his head was that it had to be an actual troll.

Gunner finally looked up and noticed the troll standing in front of him as he quickly raised his Sig Sauer and pulled the trigger. Now, if he had real military training and had been an actual war veteran, he would probably have known he had left the safety on.

The creature reached out and ripped the rifle from his grip and tossed it aside. Before Gunner could pull out his sidearm, the troll struck. Clamping its jaws around his right shoulder as warm blood spurted out

in the warm illumination of his light that now lay on the floor next to
him. The creature yanked Gunner into the darkness and they were gone.
Troy could still hear the wet crunching and slurping noises as it continued to eat his friend.

Troy screamed and turned on his Maglite and began to run the way
they came from. He immediately stopped as he saw three sets of eyes
reflecting in the glow of his flashlight.

"Fuck!" he spat as he turned and ran down the right corridor towards
the flickering light.

Booth just dropped his dog toy, tilted his head, and seemed to not
quite understand. He seemed to be wondering why Troy was running
away from him.

"Maybe it's a way out," Troy said to himself in a panic.

As the light got closer, he ran harder. He came to a complete halt
when the corridor led him into another large room. The flickering glow
he now realized was from what looked like two dozen computer screens
of all various sizes. The large stone room was filled with computer
workstations like you would find at an internet cafe.

Just like Gunner's, he thought to himself.

However, in front of each computer screen sat a troll. Each one was
unique, with different proportions. Some were lanky and hunched over,
while others looked short and squat. A few of them had long faces with
pointy noses and some had fat heads with flat noses. All of them turned
to look at him as he stood there, immobilized by terror, trying to catch
his breath. A couple of the creatures even wore headphones and appeared to be playing military first-person shooter games. One of them
took a sip out of a giant-sized styrofoam cup and made a slurping noise
that broke the silence as they all looked at him with no expression whatsoever.

Troy fumbled for the pistol in his shorts pocket that had been awkwardly slowing him down the entire time. Before he could retrieve the
pistol, two ice-cold hands reached out from behind him and rested on
his shoulders. He could see the black claws tapping themselves on his

collarbones as he closed his eyes and began to cry. He could smell his own feces fill up his cargo shorts as his bowels let loose.

"Boomeeeer," a raspy voice growled from behind him.

EPILOGUE:

One year later…

Kimberly Franklin stood in the kitchen of her $4000 a month apartment in San Francisco California scrolling through her phone as she waited for her French press to finish brewing her coffee.

Why is it all you right-wing nuts are so against gun reform? Why is it America has far more mass shootings than any other country? She viciously typed away on her phone.

She was commenting on a news article on the New York Times website in regards to a mass shooting that just happened a few days prior in Atlanta, GA.

"ARRGGGH!" she belted in frustration.

Her wife, Sandy, walked into the kitchen and retrieved a coffee mug from a cabinet.

"Why do you torture yourself with all this social media?" she asked Kimberly.

"Because! These assholes need to be told and put in their place!" she responded in a frustrated tone.

After pushing down the plunger of the French press, Sandy poured them both a cup of rich Costa Rican coffee. Holding the cup up to her nose, she paused before answering.

"There's no point. You are not going to change anyone's mind or fix the world by commenting on someone's post on social media. Besides, why can't you just accept the fact that people can have a difference of opinion? It is okay to disagree with someone," she said and took a satisfying drink of coffee.

All you racist assholes are the same. Eventually, your generation will all die off and hopefully, the world will start becoming a better place. Kimberly frantically typed while ignoring what Sandy said.

"Sometimes you infuriate me," she responded and left the kitchen.

Sandy had a heavy day of patients at her pediatrician's clinic and would probably not be home until late. Kimberly said she was back-logged at work and had to get all the coding done by the close of business, so she, too, would probably be running late. Kimberly and Sandy said their morning goodbyes, and both went their separate ways to start their day.

Kimberly got into her Prius and, before leaving the carport, she checked her phone. She had made a post on one of her social media platforms and wanted to see if anyone replied. The post was in regards to the current situation in the Ukraine. She had expressed her support for the country's people and condemned their invaders.

She had the usual supporting comments from friends and family, as she expected. There was, however, a new comment from someone she did not recognize.

Oh, look... is the little Millennial a military expert now??? The comment read.

She rolled her eyes, clicked off her phone, and left to start her day.

She arrived at a local Starbucks around 8 am. Like she did most days. She walked in, ordered a latte sat down at a table and chairs, and retrieved her laptop. Kimberly had not told Sandy yet that she had lost her job last week. They fired her for misusing the internet after being warned several times. The young progressive had a serious addiction to social media of all forms. She would frequent news sites, YouTube, Twitter, Facebook, Instagram, and many more forums and blogs. Anyone who seemed to disagree with her political views or lifestyle choices easily triggered her.

Every morning she came to the coffeehouse with the intent of sending out resumes and checking for new job listings in the tech industry.

Kimberly figured that if she could line up a new job, she could then break the news to Sandy about losing her previous job. However, she was not able to get much work done because she was always triggered by something and would spend most of her time firing back rebuttals to what she called "red hat-wearing nut jobs."

Before logging onto her computer, her phone began to vibrate frantically with notifications.

"Jesus, what the hell?" she said to herself as she opened her phone.

Someone had replied to her latest comment on the New York Times's website.

Are you going to find a job today Kimberly... or are you going to protest that too until the government does it for you??? The comment stated.

This made her skin flush instantly. Before responding, she checked the name of the person who left the comment and it read: *Troy Arlington.*

2250 SEMINOLE STREET

After months of negotiations, Stephen and Beverly Anderson pulled into the driveway of their new home at 2250 Seminole Street. Still, in their SUV, they gazed upon their new purchase with joy, pride, and a small amount of fear. This was their home now, and there was no turning back.

The Tudor Revival style home was located in Indian Village, Detroit. A historical neighborhood that is traced back to the early 20th century offering upperclass housing to many of Detroit's higher echelon classes. This particular home was one of the smaller listings in the neighborhood, being a measly 4600 square feet containing six bedrooms and bathrooms. The young couple was able to purchase the house for 550,000 dollars, which for the current market in Michigan was a steal.

"She's gorgeous, Steve," Beverly said with tears in her eyes.

"I know, right? I can't believe she belongs to us now. What year did you say they built her?" he asked in response.

"1917, is what our agent said. That makes her over a hundred years old," she said.

"Wanna go inside?" Stephen said while jingling the keys to their new home. "The moving company won't be here for another hour."

She quickly nodded like a little girl, still trying to hold back her tears. With excitement, they both exited the vehicle and made their way to the front door. With a turn of the key, the deadbolt unlocked filling their stomachs with butterflies.

"You ready for this?" he asked his wife.

Impatiently, she motioned for him to open it. The hardwood creaked as the door slowly swung open, offering them a gateway to historic luxury. Beverly held both her hands up against her mouth as she tried to contain her joy. This was the first time she had seen the home in person. Her busy work schedule didn't allow her the time to do a walkthrough, and she trusted her husband to make the call.

He looked at his wife with a sense of achievement. Then he took a deep breath and placed his arm around her. She looked up at him with puffy eyes.

"Amazing isn't it? The pictures do not do it justice," Stephen said as they both took in their surroundings.

The house had beautiful cherry wood floors that ran throughout the entire house. An enormous stone fireplace was the focal point of the main living room, giving the area a much more regal appearance. In the kitchen were massive granite countertops with all the updated modern appliances. They held each other's hands as they walked through their new home together.

A large moving truck with the words "Junk Hunks" pulled up to the curb and beeped its horn. The couple raced downstairs to greet the moving company and begin the arduous task of figuring out where things would go. In a matter of minutes, the moving crew began slogging away as box after box entered the home. Stephen just remained out of the way while his wife stood in the foyer and directed where each one should go. A young man stopped while carrying a box labeled "kitchen".

"How old is your daughter?" the young mover asked.

Beverly just looked at him and tilted her head.

"What?" she asked.

"Your daughter. I saw her peeking through the window upstairs at us as we brought boxes in," he said as she looked at him with a blank expression.

"We don't have kids," Stephen said, butting in.

"Yet," she replied.

"Ok, well, that's odd. We all swore we saw a kid looking out your window. She had blonde hair and a white dress on," he said, then placed the box where it belonged.

The couple looked at each other in bewilderment and turned back to the mover.

"Probably was just a ghost. It would be our luck if this place was haunted," Beverly said with a chuckle.

"Yeah, you are probably right," the mover responded, scratching his head.

It took the movers about two hours to get everything out of the large moving truck and into the Anderson's new home. Soon after that, Stephen made a quick trip to the hardware store while Beverly stayed at the house trying to organize the disaster that was left behind. She figured she would start in the basement and work her way up.

Beverly reached up to pull the chain that activated a light switch. With a simple click, its warm glow brought the wooden steps into visibility. Sweat began to poke through the skin of her palms. The little girl inside her was terrified of basements. She mentally stomped her foot and stood up straight in defiance. Then, with a laugh, she choked that fearful little girl down inside her and continued down the stairs.

The room was partially finished. Some of the areas had drywall while others were still brick. Then she set the box with the rest that the movers had brought down. Standing there, she scratched her head and wondered where to begin.

Leaning up against the brick in the far corner of the basement, something caught her eye. It appeared to be a picture frame, or possibly a mirror. Whatever it was looked to be about thirty by forty inches in size. She walked over, wondering what it could be.

"Well, that's not ours," she said to herself. Then she climbed through piles of cardboard boxes to get to this new object.

She reached out and turned the frame around to see what was on the other side. What she found was a heavily aged oil painting. Beverly lifted it up to look at it. It was hard to see in the dimly lit cellar, so she rushed upstairs so quickly that she almost tripped herself.

When Steve returned home from the hardware store, he found his wife sitting in the living room on their couch surrounded by unpacked boxes. Beverly hadn't moved for at least an hour since she came upstairs with her new obsession. Without taking her eyes off the canvas, she sat sipping a warm cup of herbal tea. She didn't even look up when her husband walked into the room.

"Hey babe? Whatcha doin'?" he asked with a raised eyebrow.

"Oh, hi. How long have you been standing there? Never mind, look what I found in the basement," she said while pointing a finger at what sat up against the stone fireplace.

"You found this?" he asked, then kneeled down to get a closer look.

The crusty old painting depicted a red-colored male satyr throwing its arms up in the air. A creature with the legs of a goat and the top half of a man. White paint covered its face. Outlining its skull and upper jaw. It resembled a Day of The Dead sugar skull. Two small misshapen horns twisted and turned out of its bald head.

The ears were pointed and its yellow eyes seemed way too life-like for Stephen. To him, it resembled a cross between some kind of pudgy demon and a voodoo priest. Some artists might have painted this scene as jovial, but it was not rendered that way in this particular piece.

The pallet was dark. It was neither pastel nor primary. Heavy brushstrokes caused the canvas to have its own topography. Reds, yellows, and oranges sharply contrasted with deep blacks and crisp whites. It was a very rustic-looking piece of folk art that had clearly been long forgotten.

The satyr seemed to be dancing along the banks of a river. Skeletons and bones were scattered around its hooved feet. The river ran red, and the sky was painted the color of night. A huge crescent moon and stars shining brightly created an internal light source. Stephen felt it depicted more of an evil ritual than a celebration.

"If I had to guess, I would say it's original. By the condition the paint is in, I would say it's over a hundred years old," Beverly said with a smile.

Yeah, who painted it? Clive Barker? He quietly thought as he just stared at it.

To say he was at a loss for words would be inconceivable. Sure, the painting was very well done, but its subject didn't leave much to be desired. He began to fear his wife was going to want to hang it on the wall.

"Let's put it above the fireplace. It's a serious part of Detroit's history. I believe that's the Nain Rouge," she said while obvious obsession set in.

"What the hell is a Nain Rouge?" Stephen asked.

"Well… It's an old tail that is based in Detroit folklore. It's more commonly called the Red Devil," she said while trying to recall the story. "I believe this painting is depicting the legend of the Battle of Bloody Run. Which took place in 1763. Story has it that fifty-eight British soldiers were killed by Native Americans from Chief Pontiac's Ottawa Tribe. It is said that the Nain Rouge, or Red Devil, was seen dancing among their corpses along the Detroit River as it flowed red with the soldiers' blood."

"Eh… Okay, isn't that kinda morbid?" Stephen questioned.

"Oh yeah. It's so cool. There are tons of Facebook groups and blogs about this Red Devil all over the internet. They even hold a festival once a month in the city," she responded. "Oh, please let me hang it above the fireplace. Pretty please?" Her eyes were as big as water basins.

"Happy wife, happy life. Sure," Stephen said with a sigh.

The next day, Stephen hung the ghastly painting above the mantel on the fireplace. He took a step back to make sure it was straight. He instantly noticed how much it didn't really tie the room together. Something seemed odd, though. He could have sworn the Red Devil thing was facing the other way when his wife had first discovered the picture.

"That's odd," he said to himself.

The hairs on the back of his neck began to stand on end the longer he stared. He couldn't put his finger on it, but there was something just plain wrong with it. Beverly was so excited to find this "piece of history," he didn't want to disappoint her and somehow accidentally throw it in the garbage.

The doorbell rang, causing him to jump out of his trance and let out a sheepish yelp. Collecting himself, he looked around to make sure no one saw.

When Steve opened the front door, a young couple greeted him. The woman was holding a casserole dish, and they both sported warm smiles.

"Howdy neighbor!" the man said. "My name is Paul Dini, and this is my wife, Helen."

"I made you a casserole," the woman said, beaming with joy.

"Well, that is very nice of you two. My name is Stephen Anderson and my wife Beverly is around here somewhere. Won't you two please come in?" he asked.

The couple entered their neighbor's new home and stood in the living room as Stephen took the casserole dish and walked it into the kitchen.

"Who was at the door?" Beverly called out from another room.

"Come meet our new neighbors, honey," Stephen answered in return.

Paul and Helen stood in the living room, and they both seemed to notice the painting above the fireplace. Quickly, they glanced at each other, and then back at the painting.

"Well, that's interesting," Helen said, about the artwork.

"Hey there! I'm Beverly," she said as she bounced into the room.

"Oh, hello," the man responded. "I'm Paul and this is my wife Helen. We live right next door. Figured we would come over and say hi."

"I have to be honest. We've been dying to see what the inside of this place looked like for years," Helen said. "It's a gorgeous home."

"Aw thank you," Beverly responded. "It's really like a dream come true. Excuse the mess. We are still unpacking, but please have a seat. Would you like something to drink?" She then motioned to her husband.

The couple sat down on whatever furniture wasn't covered in cardboard. When Stephen returned, he handed them both bottled water.

"I'm afraid that's all we have right now. You will have to come by another time for some wine or a cold beer," he said as he flopped down on the couch next to his wife. He noticed the couple staring above the mantel.

"Interesting piece, isn't it?" Stephen asked.

"Yeeaah... where did you get that?" Helen asked in response.

"I found it sitting in the basement," Beverly said.

She stood up and walked over to the painting as if she was drawn to it. With her right hand, she touched the canvas, feeling the brush strokes on her fingertips. Stephen watched her with curiosity and thought this was odd.

"Well, it definitely is interesting, to say the least," Paul said.

They watched Beverly stand in front of it, completely lost in thought. The other three just looked at each other for a minute, then back at Beverly.

"I believe it depicts the Nain Rouge and the Battle Of Bloody Run," she said without blinking. "How could someone leave something so beautiful behind?"

"Eh, yeah, beautiful isn't exactly the word I was looking for," Stephen said with a raised eyebrow. "Anyhow... how long have you and Helen lived here, Paul?"

Paul and Helen glanced at each other as if to remember the correct date. They paused and thought for a minute while Beverly still stood in front of the painting.

"Three years I think?" Paul wondered. "We moved in during the pandemic and that seems like yesterday, but it has been close to three years."

"Yeah, I get that. I still feel like last year was 2019," Stephen responded.

"Did you meet the people that lived here before us?" Beverly said while her eyes were still fixated on the composition in front of her.

"Actually, no. We did not," Helen said while glancing at Paul. "This was empty when we moved here and has stayed that way since."

"The neighborhood hasn't told us anything about this house. They seem to want to avoid the subject whenever we ask," Paul pointed out.

"Odd," Stephen said. "Hey, why don't we show you guys around?"

They all turned to Beverly to wait for an answer. She was still fixated on that painting above the mantel.

"Babe?" Stephen pressed.

Paul and Helen looked at each other side-eyed.

"I'm sorry. Yes, let's show you around," Beverly responded after breaking out of whatever deep thought she was in. "This place is amazing. Wait till you see the master bath."

For the next three days, Stephen and Beverly worked hard to unbox their lives and get settled into their new home. Stephen did most of the heavy lifting while Beverly walked behind him and directed where she wanted everything to go. He noticed that she still seemed to have a hard time focusing on anything other than that horrible picture in the living room. This was starting to bother him. He was letting it go for now because everything around them was still fresh and new. Sooner or later he knew he was going to have to say something because it was not normal behavior of her to be so hyper-focused on that painting.

After the last box was empty and broken down for recycling, they both took a moment to stand back. This was their new home surrounding them. Beverly began to get misty-eyed over the victory the day had brought them.

"We did it," she said and exhaled a breath.

"We sure as shit did," he responded. "Damn, look at the time. It's almost midnight. We should probably try to get some sleep."

"God, yes. I feel like I could sleep for a few days after all this. Between the physical activity and the mental exhaustion of realizing this is our new life," Beverly said.

She kissed him on the cheek and went up to bed.

Stephen waited for her to go upstairs. After that, he walked around the house to check the doors to make sure they were locked and turn out whatever lights were left on. He stopped once more in the living room and looked at that awful thing above the fireplace.

What was it about this stupid painting that has Bev so enamored with it? He thought to himself.

That's when he noticed that the red figure was now sitting down. Looking right at him from inside the picture. Now he knew he wasn't going "that" crazy and could have sworn it was originally dancing when they first discovered it. A chill ran across his entire body as he heard a voice call out from behind him.

"Stephen," something whispered.

He jumped at the sound and spun around. There, standing behind him, was a twelve-year-old girl in a white evening gown. She had long blonde hair and her entire form seemed to go in and out of focus. It was like he was watching a television set that didn't quite have the reception dialed in.

"Stephen," she said again.

The ghost's voice seemed distant. Even though it appeared to be standing in the same room, it sounded like it was coming from far away.

He reached out to touch her and his hand passed right through her body as she seemed to flicker with static. He tried one more time to touch her, and the same thing happened. It was like she was glitched.

"He's coming for her," she said.

Stephen awoke the next morning, relieved to learn that the night before was just a dream. He looked at his cell phone and noticed that it said 6 am. His wife was gone and he was alone.

He quickly got up and went downstairs. There, on the floor in front of the fireplace, sat his wife. She sat there just staring up at that God-awful picture. He wondered how long she had been up since it was already so early.

"Bev?" he quietly asked.

She didn't reply and continued to stare. The Nain Rouge was seated like in his dream and it faced her with a smile. She was lost in its gaze.

"Bev? Babe?" he asked, a little louder now.

She was once again transfixed by its pull. There was something inside the painting and it was clear to her that it wanted out. She felt as if she could be the key.

"BABE!" he yelled.

Beverly jumped back and was startled to see Stephen standing there in the living room. A very concerned expression shaped his face.

"Hey Stephen," she said playfully. "Whatcha doing?"

This odd response confused him for a minute. He just wrinkled his brow and looked befuddled.

"Oh, I'm just joking around you big ding dong," she said with a smirk.

"What the? What do you mean 'joking' around?" he asked as she stood up.

"Is there any coffee yet?" she asked.

Stephen's mouth hung open as his wife just pranced by him like they were playing a game. He looked back at the painting. The Nain Rouge was now back to what he thought was its original position when they discovered it.

"That's odd," he commented.

Between his dream last night and now this. He could tell today was going to be interesting.

Beverly acted odd for the remainder of the day. She was being far too carefree and almost childish. She bounced around the house in a bubbly manner, laughing and carrying on. If he didn't know any better, he would think she was stoned.

"Hey babe?" he asked.

She was twirling like a ballerina through the kitchen with a spray bottle of cleaner. Wiping little spots here and there.

"What's that, my love?" she said with whimsical spirit.

"Don't get me wrong. I love what you got going on here, but are you… high?" he asked bashfully.

"Ha! No silly." She shooed at him. "If anything, I'm high on the thought of the life we are going to build here. I'm just excited, that's all."

Stephen accepted her response with a cockeyed grin. He thought this was horseshit because she would never, ever act like this. She had a sense of humor, but she was always very mature for her age. Being playful was not something he had ever seen her do.

"Alright then," he said and slowly walked away from her.

Stephen stood in the kitchen and looked at the living room. Between his wife acting weird, last night's dream, and the sudden interest in the Nain Rouge, something was off. He was ruminating on the fact none of this started before finding that grotesque monstrosity. He didn't know how yet, but he was going to find it.

For the rest of the day, Stephen sat with his face buried in his laptop screen. He was Googling and searching for anything related to the history of their house along with the legends of the Nain Rouge. There was far more information than he expected.

Hundreds of links appeared for the Nain Rouge, and he figured the majority of it was bullshit. The information about the house he found was very interesting. It appeared that during the 106-year lifespan of the home, there had been seventeen murders. The cases were all similar. They were committed by someone in the household.

In 1932, a father was believed to have killed his wife and son. The man was a beloved member of the community and ended up slicing his wife and infant son's aortas while they slept. His teenage daughter escaped the house and returned with the police. A two-hour standoff occurred which led to the father being shot to death by the authorities.

In 1969, a small boy waited till his father left for work before he took his mother's life. The nine-year-old boy drove knitting needles into her ears while she relaxed in the bathtub. When the father returned home, he quickly called the police. Before the police arrived, the father killed his son with a ball-peen hammer in self-defense.

Stephen found more murders that had occurred in their home that spanned over the next few decades. He wished the real estate agent had disclosed this information to them before they closed. Then Stephen recognized the little girl from his dream. She went missing in 1996 along with the rest of her family. They all just seemed to vanish without a trace.

He slowly raised his eyes from his laptop and looked across the room to the painting above the mantel. Regardless if everything was just a coincidence or not, he was going to have a long talk with Beverly tomorrow morning and the painting was going in the trash.

Beverly got up around 2 am and left her husband snoring by himself on their queen-sized bed. The stairs lightly squeaked under each of her feet. She tip-toed across the first floor and into the living room. There she clicked on the Tiffany lamp that sat next to the couch and sat down and waited for her eyes to adjust.

She smiled and pulled her legs up Indian style as she sat on the couch. It was as if the painting had called her down. There was something it wanted to tell her. Some kind of secret that only she would know.

A low hum began to ring in her ears.

Beverly reflexively stuck her pinky in one of her ears to correct anything that might be causing her to hear this droning. Meanwhile, she couldn't keep her eyes off the painting. Reds and oranges seemed to swirl in front of her. It was as if the river was flowing across the canvas.

The hum now became a much louder rumble.

She tried to stick her finger in her ear once more, but she couldn't. She could move her eyes, but nothing else on her body responded to what she wanted it to do. Her eyes darted around the room, looking for something that could help her. Panic was now blazing across the highways of her brain.

The loud rumble now became a deep roar.

Even though Beverly found herself unable to move, she could still feel. The sweat that was now soaking into her nightgown and beading up on her forehead gave her a cooling sensation. This let her know that she wasn't completely paralyzed. However, she quickly realized that she could also still feel pain.

The roar stopped and everything went quiet.

In a flash, her head snapped back and forced her to look straight up at the ceiling. The pain was excruciating. As if her head was being yanked from her body by an unknown force. Every tendon and vertebrae overextended itself and sent daggers to her pain receptors throughout her brain. A tear ran down her cheek as she tried to push a scream out. She couldn't.

Her mouth forced itself open so far it dislocated. There was nothing she could do but feel every inch of her body rampaging with agony. She could still look at the ceiling, but that was becoming difficult as her eyes watered heavily from the pain.

A warm jet of air blew past her gums and pushed itself down her throat. Forcing itself through her windpipe and into her lungs. She was completely defenseless and immobile. All she could do was take in the pain and wait for it to be over.

The ceiling was now completely out of focus to her. A series of massive convulsions took over her body as if it were being pushed to its physical limits.

Beverly was trapped inside her body, fighting to keep control of what she had left. Blackness began to surround her peripheral vision. Slowly, something made its way inside her as the void closed in.

Then, just like that, the pain was gone.

The Nain Rouge looked at itself in the reflection of the refrigerator. Beverly had great skin. She had a nice body too. It was very pleased with this. The demon always found that pretty people could get their way much easier than those who were not.

Something was wrong, though.

It opened one of the drawers in the kitchen and looked around the contents as a painter would look through their brushes. This vessel lacked depth. It needed to change that. Finally, it settled on a paring knife.

"This will do nicely," it said.

Returning to Beverly's reflection, the small knife made an incision just below her scalp. It began to drag the knife straight across her hairline, causing the skin to separate as if it unzipped. Warm blood drizzled down her forehead and over the bridge of her nose. Beverly smiled at herself as the Nain Rouge pulled the knife down to her earlobe. More blood slowly dripped onto the tile floor. The knife then ran under her cheekbone and over to her nose. It then outlined the right side of her maxilla and brought the knife down to her upper jaw.

With both hands, it slowly began to slice through her upper lip, and carefully removed it up to the septum. This now exposed her upper teeth and gums. It let the small hunks of meat drop to the floor. It then regarded itself once more in the reflection of the stainless steel appliance. Slowly, it peeled her skin away, leaving only her mandible intact. Her subcutaneous tissue was exposed from her hairline down. All that remained was a grotesque, disfigured horror.

It wiggled her nose, then thought for a minute. That useless chunk of cartilage had to go.

Stephen had fallen asleep on the bed upstairs, reading articles on his tablet about the house. These went into more detail about the murders that occurred over the decades. In each case, one family member remained alive or was never found.

"Stephen," a voice quietly whispered.

He was suddenly pulled from his sleep. There at the base of the bed stood the young girl from his dreams.

"Stephen, it's here. You can't let it get out." The child said with a sense of urgency.

"What? What's here?" he asked, still dazed from just waking up.

"It can't leave the house until it sacrifices all who live here," she explained.

"What?" he muttered.

"It cannot escape from its prison until it kills you, Stephen. Once that happens, he will be free to come and go as he pleases," she frantically explained.

"Honey," Beverly's voice called out from down the hallway.

"You can't let it leave," the child repeated.

He shot out of bed and slammed the bedroom door. Then he scrambled for something to use as a weapon. Even though this all seemed like a baffling fever dream, he still felt the need to protect himself.

Her footsteps caused the wood to sag and creak down the hallway ever so slightly as it drew near the bedroom.

"Stephen… It's snuggle time," his wife purred.

Stephen hurried into the master bath looking for anything he could use as a weapon. He decided to yank the towel bar free from the wall. He stopped and looked at himself in the mirror. There, he realized that this was stupid. His wife needed his help.

"What the fuck am I doing?" he asked himself.

He threw the towel bar down on the bathroom counter and made his way back to the bedroom.

This is all crazy. There was no ghost child and my wife wasn't possessed by some evil being, He thought as he walked over to the bedroom door.

When he opened the door, he envisioned Beverly would be standing there. She was. Except it wasn't the Bev he had seen hours ago. Stephen took a step back and looked on with complete shock.

He placed his hands over his mouth. If this was a dream, it was now a nightmare.

The paring knife had removed most of her skin. The result revealed bone, tendons, and ichor. Beverly's top row of teeth and gums were now exposed. Just like the little red demon in the painting, it resembled the white skull makeup. It even went so far as to remove his wife's nose and eyebrows.

Eyes wide with madness, she tilted her head and watched him. She pursed her lower lip as if trying to pout. He could see her face glisten as blood oozed down her chin. He began to cry at the sight of his once-beautiful wife. She had permanently disfigured herself.

"Hello, bunny-boo," she said playfully.

"Bev? What did you do? Oh God, what did you do?" he cried out.

"Oh? I just gave myself a quick facelift," she replied and took a step forward.

He noticed that she was holding the meat cleaver from the kitchen.

"Beverly, why are you holding that? We need to call 911 and get you some help," he pleaded.

"What, this old thing?" She looked down at the cleaver in her hand.

With startling speed, she raised the blade above her head. Before she could bring it down Stephen dove into the bathroom and slammed the door with his foot. He quickly locked the door and began to pace back and forth.

Beverly gently tapped her fingers against the door of the master bath.

Tap… tap… tap… tap…

"Stephen. Please come out dear," she said in between her gentle tapping.

He quickly realized his cellphone was on the bed.

"Stephen, please open the door," she whispered.

"We need to get you some help, Beverly. You have to let me call the paramedics," he begged while scrambling around in the bathroom.

"I'm going to carve out your heart, Stephen," she said.

Her voice was much deeper now. He knew that whatever was on the other side of this bathroom door quite possibly was no longer his Beverly. The beautiful, kind, and loving woman he admired with so much pride was no longer here.

The Nain Rouge began to beat his wife's fists against the door as it flew into a tantrum.

Paul grabbed the towel bar from off the counter and slowly approached the door. He wasn't quite sure what he was planning to do, but he had to get to a phone. He had to try for help. Thats when the doorbell rang.

Paul stood on the front porch and rang the doorbell. Helen was worried by all the noise and sent him over to check on them. There was no answer, so he pounded on the door this time. He then realized he left his cell phone on the back of their toilet.

"Who is it?" Beverly cheerfully asked from the other side of the door.

"It's Paul, your neighbor. Is everything okay?" he asked.

"Oh, everything's peachy. Would you like to come in?" she asked in return.

Back in the bathroom, Stephen had begun to climb out of the window as soon as he heard the doorbell ring. Unfortunately, the master bathroom faced the backyard. He had to warn whoever was at the front door. Quickly, he lowered himself from the gutter. Trying his best to be careful and not have it pull away from the soffits by his weight. His feet slipped, causing him to lose his balance and fall into a forsythia bush.

"Yes please," Paul replied. "Helen will not let me sleep if I don't check and make sure you guys are okay."

The door slowly opened. Paul stepped inside and looked around. Beverly remained behind the large door, out of sight. Everything looked normal until he saw the blood in the kitchen. His eyes widened, and he released an audible gasp. The kitchen sink and floor were smeared with red. He could see a set of crimson footprints make their way up the stairs.

"Don't worry. It's not Stephen's blood," she calmly said from behind him.

"Where's Stephen?" he asked frantically.

He turned around and finally saw Beverly's freshly mutilated face.

Stephen startled Paul as he came screaming up the stairs of the porch. Before Paul could turn and look towards the commotion, he noticed she was holding a meat cleaver in her hand.

"Nooo!" Stephen called out.

Beverly slammed the door on him and locked it before he could get inside.

"Beverly!" he yelled as he banged on the door. "Paul, you have to run!"

He could hear his neighbor scream from inside as Beverly buried the meat cleaver into Paul's forehead with a loud thwack.

Stephen paced. Trying to remember what it was the little girl said to him.

Something about it can't leave the house until it kills everyone that lives here? He remembered.

The door slowly opened.

"Hey there, bunny-boo," Beverly said. "Why don't you come back inside?"

On the floor, in a pool of blood behind her, he could see Paul's body. His legs still twitched as the last of his life drained out onto the floor.

Maybe Paul's still alive, he thought. He hesitated for a moment, still unsure.

"That's it. Why don't you come back inside?" she asked again.

Stephen noticed the little girl was now standing with him on the porch. She had a sad look on her face.

"You have to run Stephen!" she pleaded. "You cannot go inside. Please, I beg you, do not go back inside."

"Don't listen to that little brat," Beverly snipped.

"The Nain Rouge was imprisoned here almost a century ago, Stephen. You must run. Get as far as you can. This house should burn to the ground," the apparition explained.

"But she's my wife and I have to help her," he responded.

"Yes. I need your help, Stephen. Please come inside and sit down and we can talk all this out. You know, like 'adults'," she formed air quotes with her fingers.

"Don't go in there, Stephen," the child pleaded one last time.

This was his wife. The woman he swore his life to. She was also his best friend, and he loved her more than anything in the world. All he wanted to do was scoop her up into his arms and tell her everything was going to be okay while they waited for the police to arrive. He would get her the medical treatment she needed and would be right by her side.

"I'm sorry, I have to help her," Stephen said as he entered the house.

"Run Stephen! You have to resist!" the child yelled.

"I can't. I won't just leave her like this," he muttered as he looked at the disfigured shell that had once been his partner.

Beverly smiled at him as he walked through the front door. She then closed the door behind him.

Stephen felt a heavy impact come down on the back of his head. It was all so fast he didn't fully understand what had happened to him. Too disoriented to sense any pain, he turned to look at what he thought was still some shred of his wife.

"There, that wasn't so hard, was it?" he heard Beverly's voice say.

His vision became blurry, and he felt like he was floating. He still couldn't exactly figure out what was going on. Why was he so tired all of a sudden? He began to stumble as he took a step towards her.

"Yes, now come here and give me a hug," the demon said with a smile.

Stephen's legs gave out, and he fell forward onto his knees, then collapsed to the floor face first.

Everything was slowly going black as he heard Beverly's footsteps come closer. He still couldn't quite process what exactly was going on.

The Nain Rouge placed his wife's barefoot on the back of Stephen's head. Applying just enough pressure with her arch to hold him still, it dislodged the cleaver from his skull.

Helen sat in her living room with her television on mute. She had been texting Paul for a half hour now. Trying to get a response that everything was okay. Worry had already long set in. It wasn't like him to not answer a text right away. She knew something was wrong. Her stomach danced and turned uncontrollably.

"Damnit Paul, where are you?" she cursed.

She couldn't doom scroll on her phone any longer. There was nothing positive to keep her mind from expecting the worst. Not even cat videos were working.

They had not known Stephen and Beverly for very long. She didn't have any bad feelings about the couple, so she wasn't worried they would hurt Paul in any way.

But, we really don't know them all that well, she thought.

Helen figured that they should all probably get together for dinner soon. She could cook and they could bring whatever they liked. Get to know each other. Maybe Paul would even break out his dominos and teach them how to play a game called Mexican Train.

That was as long as neither of their new neighbors turned out to be an axe murderer.

"Maybe some warm tea will help calm me down?" she said, then stood up and walked into the kitchen.

She filled her teakettle up with tap water and placed it on the quick boil burner on her stove. The igniter clicked until it lit and blue flames danced around the bottom of the kettle.

She retrieved a mug from the cupboard and calmly waited for the whistle. In the meantime, she impatiently checked her phone to make sure she didn't miss anything from Paul.

There was a sudden knock at the door that startled her.

"Jesus!" she spat.

The anxiety was becoming too much for her.

"Helen, it's me, Beverly," a voice said.

"Beverly, where's Paul?" she asked while walking towards the door.

"I'm hurt bad… Can you let me in?" Beverly responded.

"Oh my God, yes. Please come in," Helen said as she placed her hand on the doorknob.

Back at 2250, the front door was left wide open. Both Stephen and Paul had been placed upright in the living room furniture. They were both sat facing the mantle. Like two unwanted marionettes with the strings removed. Their faces were completely void of life.

Helen's screams bounced off the walls as they came through the open doorway.

Beverly had seen everything from within the painting. She was now part of the oils and the pigments on the canvas. When the demon entered her body, it swapped places with her soul. Now she was trapped in between the planes of existence for eternity.

Beverly couldn't scream, nor could she call for help. All she could do was watch.

I CAN'T LET YOU IN

Viola Ruth was a sixty-eight-year-old proud evangelical. She prided herself on being a "good" Christian and doing everything that came along with that self-proclaimed title. She and her husband Frank moved to this specific neighborhood about forty years ago for that reason. It was a good Christian community.

It sickened her sometimes.

Everyone here really looked out for each other. Taking care of one's neighbor was the good Christian thing to do. So everyone at Paradise Grove's gated community was kind and caring. It was her life-long dream to live among people of the right faith.

She never trusted anyone.

They would have potlucks on Sundays, and the mothers would rotate for daycare. Family gatherings were a weekly thing when they were not all in church. It was a warm and happy place where she and her husband raised a family.

The little shits didn't deserve anything.

Viola nervously paced their living room, continuously peeking through the blinds towards the street. She was expecting to see someone walk up their sidewalk. She just wasn't sure why, though.

Her husband, Frank, sat slumped over in his chair as a rerun of Jeopardy played on the television. In front of him was a cold bowl of Dinty Moore Beef Stew. His TV tray was scattered with green peas that he had picked meticulously out of his dinner.

Just disgusting.

This drove Viola nuts. It was like he had the diet of a twelve-year-old boy. One day, she would get him to eat something green.

Drip. Drip. Drip... said the kitchen sink that Frank had never gotten around to fixing yet.

Viola went back and forth frantically across the mustard-yellow carpeting. Her mind was racing faster than she could keep up with.

What will the neighbors think?

"In 1937, his sister said he had 'hats of every description,' which he would use as a foundation of his next book," Alex Trebek's voice said from the television.

She knew something was coming. She didn't know what form it would take, but she knew it would be here soon.

Drip. Drip. Drip... The water droplets fell into an empty saucer that lay in the bottom of the sink.

Frank let out a gurgle and flatulated as he remained slumped over in his chair.

"Frank!" Viola spat.

She was used to his flatulence, but this one was awful. It smelled like he messed himself this time.

She could feel the weight on her chest increase as the panic attack made its way towards her like a runaway train.

"Who is Dr. Seuss?" Alex Trebek asked.

Why was this happening to her? She had been a good Christian. This sort of thing didn't happen to her kind. She gave and gave each week as much as she could. With the goodness of her heart. Doing what was right by others and taking care of people's needs.

The heck with them all. You have done nothing wrong. This time.

Drip. Drip. Drip... Continued the sink in response.

She had donated so much to the church. Not just with money, but with her time. Viola had organized and helped out with all the church activities, Sunday school teachings, and even carpools. She was usually the one to always start the prayer chain for those in need.

"He's coming Viola," Alex Trebek said from the other side of the flatscreen.

Viola stopped in her tracks and looked horrified at the television. Alex Trebek was looking straight at her from his podium.

"You have to be ready, Viola. He's not going to stop until he takes him," Mr. Trebek said.

"What can I do?" She responded to the game show host.

Drip. Drip. Drip... The sound started to bore into her temples.

"You've done everything you can, honey. You can't let him in. Whatever you do. Do not let him in," Trebek responded.

There was a sudden knock at the front door.

The noise startled her, causing her to flinch. Who could it be at this hour? She rarely had guests anymore these days. She wondered if it was him. Was Alex Trebek telling her the truth?

"Who is it?!" she shouted.

"It's me. Reverend Brown," a male voice replied kindly.

Drip. Drip. Drip...

"Reverend? Is that you?" she asked in return.

A lightning bolt lit up the sky and she could see his silhouette through the curtains as a loud crack of thunder made her tense up even more at the uninvited guest's arrival.

"Do not fall for his kindness, Viola," Alex called out from inside her television.

The Reverend Brown had just moved to the neighborhood about a month prior. She had taken a shine to this young man because he resembled someone from her past. The similarity was uncanny. Before she accepted Jesus Christ as her Lord and Savior, Viola had lived a very different life. It was a time full of ill repute and experimental debauchery. Like most people, as they come into adulthood, she was floundering through her existence with no direction or purpose. It wasn't until she met a man of the cloth in 1978 that she found her way towards God. The new preacher reminded her of this man very much, and she liked that.

Brown always seemed to work long hours at the church and she would see him only at night. Either at nightly sermons or midnight masses. Sometimes she would see him come home late at night with his three boys.

Those boys were always up there with their daddy when he was spreading the good of the gospel to the folks of the community. The boys would also help everyone at church and were just the kindest of little ones. At times she wished her two sons were as nice as the Reverend's.

Instead, I got two grown up assholes.

The Reverend had been weighing heavily on the Rapture and the Great Tribulation in his recent sermons. Though Viola identified as a devoted Christian, she had begun to worry that her husband may not be.

She was afraid that even though Frank was a good man, he hadn't fully accepted Jesus Christ as his Savior. He more or less saw the words of the bible as a teaching tool on how to live your life to be a better person. Frank wasn't worried about being the best Christian per se but was more interested in just being a good person overall. Viola had a firm belief that the world would end soon and that those who were not taken up to heaven would remain on earth during the Great Tribulation. They would be forced to wear the mark of the beast. Those with the mark would be sent to hell for eternity for not accepting Jesus Christ into their lives.

This constantly ran through her mind. Day after day and night after night. This caused her to remain in a constant state of anxiety and worry. She was terrified that she and her husband would not be together in Heaven and bask in the warm glow of the Lord.

A few days after Brown's last sermon, the numbers 0110 0110 0110 showed up on the back of her husband's left hand. Now here the Reverend was at her door in the middle of the night. Asking if she would let him and his boys in.

P lease, Viola. Let us in. We know how you feel," the Reverend said with sincerity.

"Hogwash!" she spat back through the door while she continued to pace.

Drip. Drip. Drip...

"I can help you," the Reverend said politely.

"No, he can't, Viola. He's lying to you," Alex Trebek said in response to the Reverend.

She looked at her husband, then back at the door. Viola was becoming more agitated. Her hands moved frantically through the air as she spoke. Like she was conducting some mad, intense piece of classical music.

"I can't let you in. I won't let you in. I won't!" she bellowed.

"Yes, Viola. Keep it up. Drive him back into the night." Mr. Trebek supported her confidence.

Viola noticed she had bitten her right thumbnail down so far she was starting to bleed.

"You need us. We came to help you. Everything will be okay if you just let us in," he repeated softly.

Drip. Drip. Drip...

Goshdarnet! Frank, why haven't you fixed that sink?

"I can't let you near my husband! I won't let you in!" She yelled, pointing a finger towards the door.

Suddenly, she could see movement outside her front window. It looked like Reverend Brown's boys were running around looking for something. She could see them in their little black rain coats. They had their hoods up, keeping their faces in the shadows and obstructed from her view.

Every time she would look for one, they were gone. They seemed to dart back and forth through every window in her living room.

"Make sure the back door is secure!" Mr. Trebek reminded Viola.

She ran across the living room and reached the back door wall to fasten the lock. She peaked through the curtain, but all she saw was rain. Then noticed tiny oily handprints on the glass about waist height.

"Good job, Viola." Alex Trebek praised her courageously.

She scurried back across the living room floor and back to the front door. Tears were welling up inside her eyes, but she was determined to keep her husband safe.

"You will not enter this home, Reverend Brown," Viola said with a low growl and stood her ground.

Drip. Drip. Drip…

"Oh, come on. Please show some respect." The Reverend said back with a sarcastic tone.

In a flash of lightning, she caught a glimpse of one of the boys. It terrified her beyond her wildest nightmare. The boy's skin was a grayish color and his eyes and mouth were sewn shut with black wiring. The thing pressed its hands and face against the windowpane, then just like that, it was gone.

She let out a scream at the sight of the little demonic thing. She could tell that it seemed to be searching for another access inside.

"They are trying to get in Viola," Mr. Trebek said in the background.

"No. No. No. No," she sobbed, then turned her back to the wall next to the television and slid down to the floor. She was starting to crack. She was strong, but this was pushing her beyond her limits of sanity and faith.

There she sat with her face planted in her palms, trying her best to keep her wits about her.

Not again. Not again. Not again.

God Damn it! You old hag! Let me in!" the Reverend spat as his temper flared. His boot kicked the bottom of the front door, giving it a loud thud.

Viola jumped at the sound, but remained seated against the wall.

"I can't let you in. I can't let you in," she repeated as she rocked back and forth.

"You fucking bitch let me in!" The Reverend screamed.

Drip. Drip. Drip...

More shadows darted to and fro just outside her windows.

There was another bash at the front door. It startled Viola. The bashing continued and got louder with each contact.

"He's going to get in, Viola. You have to be ready." Alex Trebek said.

"I CAN'T LET YOU IN!" she screamed as she stood up and faced the door. Tears ran down her face as she balled up her fists as tight as she could.

This is it...

"Open the door, you pathetic wench!" he screamed. "You call yourself a good Christian and you won't even let a man of the cloth into your own home?"

The bashing had increased to the point that the door was going to bust open. She began to look around the room as the panic set in.

Drip. Drip. Drip...

"You stupid old bitch. God doesn't love you anymore. Jesus is just a made-up story to keep brainless twerps like you in line. Did you think you would be safe here? After all these years?" the Reverend asked. "You can't hide from us. NOW OPEN THE FUCKING GODDAMN DOOR!"

The bashing continued. The front door was seconds from bursting. Viola's heart was racing, and she was finding it hard to catch her breath as the panic attack took over.

"It's time, Viola," Mr. Trebek said one last time from inside her television.

She scrambled around to do something, realizing she was out of options, so she dislodged the axe from her husband's sternum and turned to face Reverend Brown.

Two young police officers arrived at the Ruth residence around 1:30 am. The squad car's headlights tried to cut through the deluge as best they could. The rain had been coming down non-stop for hours now. With at least an attempt to stay somewhat dry, the two men put on their department issue rain ponchos. This was not the first time that the two officers had been dispatched to this residence. A concerned neighbor had called in, stating that they heard sounds of a domestic dispute.

The officers both knew and admired Frank Ruth. He was a well-respected man who still ran his small mom and pop hardware store since the 1990s. It was his wife that made them cringe. She was always seen as just a little bit off. The words "screw loose" had already been used around the precinct more than once.

The calls were usually all the same. Frank would answer the door and his wife would be screaming about some heaven and hell mumbo jumbo, cursing them up and down for not accepting the same beliefs she did. They expected tonight to end as usual, with Frank calming his wife down and apologizing for wasting the officers' time. The young men were not prepared for what the night was going to bring them.

One officer was able to peek in one of the living room windows and see what she had done to her husband. There in his chair, Frank Ruth sat covered in his own blood while their television played their favorite game show. The axe was still embedded in his chest.

To avoid further bloodshed, they tried to coax the old woman out of her home from behind the front door. After this tactic did not work, they had no choice but to force their way inside.

As the door flew inwards, they saw the sixty-eight-year-old woman with her axe held high and her eyes blazing with fury. Before she crossed the distance of her living room, both officers drew their sidearms in self-defense.

"You can't have my husband!" was the last thing Viola said.

Without hesitation, each of their pistols barked three times, putting an end to Mrs. Ruth's personal nightmare.

In the days that followed, the homicide detectives began to piece the events of that horrible night together in Paradise Grove. They found that Mrs. Ruth had once been a lead suspect in a multiple missing persons case on the East Coast from the late 70s. The authorities had discovered signs of foul play but never discovered the bodies, nor did they find what they believed to be a murder weapon. This unsolved case involved a pastor by the name of William Brown. The man, along with his three sons, had gone missing in Portsmouth, New Hampshire. The case notes stated that the last person to see them alive was a young woman by the name of Viola Ruth.

GOLDEN HANDCUFFS

The wind whistled through the treetops as broken shards of glass popped under Greg's boot as he walked up the driveway. Carefully, he inched toward an abandoned single-family ranch in a subdivision just southwest of Austin, Texas. The glass was from a busted rear window of the Lincoln Navigator that was left parked in the drive. He figured it was from looters looking for anything they could find.

It has now been a year since the world officially ended. He was not exactly sure how it started or where. That didn't matter, because now the world was a wasteland suspended in time. Greg slowly inched his way towards the front door and prayed it was unoccupied. He picked this house because other than the busted up Navigator in the driveway, it looked untouched for some time.

Greg held his Ruger 10-22 rifle at the ready as he kicked the front door twice with his boot tip. He waited a minute to listen for any movement from inside the house. There was none. Raising his right foot, he kicked in the front door with one swift, powerful motion. Quickly, he noticed the lack of decay and rot that usually attacked his olfactory senses. This told him "they" were not here. He scanned the living room as he stepped inside the home. The previous owners had decorated the house in a southwestern motif, with lots of turquoise, peach, and mauve.

Greg stepped through the house and checked each room for any survivors or threats. The home was empty and, by the looks of it, had been for many months. Greg returned to the living room, plopped on the couch with his rifle on his lap, and exhaled heavily. A calico cat meowed as it pranced through the front door and slammed its head into one of his shins. It purred as it began to rub against his leg.

"Hello, George," Greg said as he leaned down to pet his friend on the head.

Greg had no idea who George originally belonged to. George had just begun to follow Greg one day months ago while walking through a neighborhood checking houses for supplies. He noticed this male cat that came over to him right away while walking out of an empty house. The cat was overly friendly and had a collar that had the name George embroidered on it.

George came and went as he pleased, but he always tagged along and wasn't too far behind Greg as he made his way north. Greg welcomed the company since he hadn't seen a living person in about six months. Sometimes he wondered if he and George were the last two alive anywhere on the planet.

Before he got too comfortable, Greg got up and checked the house one more time. He made sure the doors were all locked and he even barricaded whatever he could with anything heavy. Closing off any access from the outside world that he could. He just needed to rest for a night and he would get moving in the morning. Greg wedged an overstuffed lazy boy against the front door and took off his rucksack and placed it on the carpet next to the couch. He laid down and tried to close his eyes as George jumped up onto his chest, curled himself up into a ball, and went fast asleep.

"Long day too buddy?" Greg asked as he gently ran his hand across the fur ball on his chest. Greg finally drifted off into a peaceful sleep.

The next morning, Greg rummaged through the kitchen cupboards and the pantry to see if there was anything he could take. Looking for anything that could be of use to him that on an average day might have been overlooked such as a can opener. He found a couple of cans of beans, which he took for himself.

"Hey look, George, you're in luck. I found some tuna," Greg said.

The cat was rubbing up against his pant legs as it heard the sound of the can opener cut into the top. He opened the tuna and laid it on the floor for George. He scratched the feline on its backside as it gorged itself. There was a roll of duct tape in a drawer, a couple of good permanent markers, and an extra can opener.

"Score!" he said as he snatched the items up.

The tri-level was pretty picked over otherwise. Whoever left here must have taken everything they thought was useful. It didn't look like the place was looted because everything was still in its place. He took one last look in the bathroom to see if there was any soap or shampoo or anything pertaining to personal hygiene. Whoever lived there apparently must have made a lot of overnight stops in hotels because there was a stockpile of small hotel soaps and shampoos in the linen closet in the hallway.

"Good haul today, George," Greg said as the cat meowed and sauntered into another room. He figured he had spent enough time looking through this family's belongings and it was time for them to get back on the road.

"One of these days, I'll come across a house that has car keys in it. It's not like I can just Google how to hot-wire a car," he muttered to himself as he hiked up his rucksack and tightened the straps to secure it in place on his back.

"Alright George, let's get moving on. You know I don't like to travel at night if we can avoid it," he said as he looked down at his partner.

George sprawled out in front of him on his back, waiting for a belly rub after its meal. Greg knelt to give the cat a scratch, then stood up and headed for the door. George quickly padded after him once he exited.

If Greg had to guess, he would say it was probably between 8 and 10 am. The birds were chirping outside and considering the world had ended a year prior, it was shaping up to be a pretty nice day. The temperature was a perfect 75 degrees without a cloud in the sky. Greg knew he shouldn't waste any time lollygagging around so after checking his compass to make sure he was heading north, he navigated his way through the middle-class subdivision. He was always careful not to get greedy. Without knowing how safe the area was, he didn't want to waste too much time going through these abandoned homes. There was only so much that he could carry and didn't see the point just yet. He wanted to stay on the move and travel light for now.

Greg liked to pace himself while traveling. On a good day, he could do 30 to 35 miles safely without tiring himself out too much for the next day. With Greg, slow and steady was the way to go. He was adamant about being aware of his surroundings at all times. Not to mention a blister on your foot could ruin your week if you pressed too hard.

If Greg had to guess, he would say he had been hiking for at least ten hours by the time he came to MoGo Mato Motors. The building was five stories high and was set on about 650 acres of property. MoGo Mato Motors was a Japanese car company that specialized in the latest cutting edge EV vehicles. All he saw now was the lifeless husk of an office building that sat by itself across a divided highway.

Greg stood just outside the entrance gate to the MoGo Mato Motors and debated with himself over whether he should go inside. Scattered across the football stadium size parking lot, he guessed there were easily two hundred or more cars. It dawned on him that each car was probably a life that had ended right here a year ago when everything fell apart.

"Well, George, this might be a great idea or a horrible idea," he said.

George just meowed and sauntered around, rubbing up against anything that was near him. Like most cats, he seemed to be most interested in showing off his anus than listening to anyone.

Greg figured that there had to be at least one set of car keys in that office building somewhere. This was going to be a daunting task. He was going to have to sweep each floor to make sure the building was clear, then go back through and look for what he could find. He had seen enough dead people since everything ended, so he was okay with that. It was just he didn't want to run into "them" while inside and boxed in.

They approached an abandoned police car that was parked just outside the front entrance of the building. The car was empty and the driver's side door was open as well as the trunk. Greg couldn't find anything of value, and it appeared that the car had already been looted for anything useful.

"Of course, no keys," Greg said to himself as he raised his Ruger and approached the foyer of the building. The front windows and doors were all shattered or cracked and covered in dried blood, bile, and grime. This made it very difficult for Greg to see into the building. The large revolving door was jammed with office furniture, so that option was out. There was a broken window that was unblocked and big enough to crawl through.

"Great," he mumbled.

All he needed was to cut his hand and get it infected. Greg kicked the door frame a few times with his boot to make a loud noise, and he slowly backed away from the opening. He held his rifle at the ready, but nothing happened. No strange noises or cries for help. Just the same dead silence he had been hearing for the past few months now.

"I'm going in, George. Wait here," Greg said to his sidekick, who paid him no attention in return. He climbed his way carefully into the lobby of the building. Whatever furniture wasn't wedged into the revolving doors was strewn all over the foyer. There was only one body in the otherwise empty room. The first thing Greg noticed was the lack of any strong odors other than mildew and mold. This body was at least a year old and was long decomposed. Reaching into his thigh pocket on his cargo pants, he retrieved a pair of latex gloves and put them on. He examined the body and saw a MoGo Mato Motors employee badge that had the name Tyler written on it.

What the hell happened here? Greg thought to himself...

GOLDEN HANDCUFFS

ONE YEAR AGO...

Chad had blindly smacked at his alarm clock as it screeched on the night-stand next to him. Drilling small pestering holes into his temples. Having hit snooze four times prior, as usual, he finally made the maddening noise stop and he crawled out of bed to start his day. The thousand-square-foot home had a hallway that was not long enough to allow Chad to wake up before he got to the kitchen. He shuffled his feet, lumbered over to Mr. Coffee, and pressed the "on" button. Chad stood there and moped while it slowly brewed its first pot of the day. Reaching into one of the cupboards he grabbed his favorite Mt T. Mug. After fumbling the half and half from the fridge, he poured a generous amount into his cup. He pondered if he really liked the taste of coffee or just coffee-flavored sugar milk. Shrugging to himself, he put two tablespoons of sugar into his cup before pouring his hot elixir of life. He squinted his eyes while he looked at the clock on the microwave and sipped his coffee. It read 6:35 am and he had to leave for work within the next ten minutes or traffic would make him late for his job.

"I hate my life," he said to himself. Then he turned around and lumbered back to his bedroom.

Chad sat in his Honda Civic in the morning rush hour traffic of I-35 on his way to work. It was your typical morning gridlock, as it was every single day. He technically only had a 25-minute commute, but with traffic, it could take up to an hour. This was especially true on any day that he left a minute after 6:45 am. Today he left at 6:43 am, which meant he would still make it on time, but he would not have his morning coffee time.

Coffee time was something you did before you started your day. Chad would come into the building, log into his computer, and then spend a good twenty or thirty minutes catching up on his numerous social media accounts as well as national and international news. Today, however, he would not be able to do that. There would be just enough time for him to clock in and start taking supervisor calls as soon as he got to his cubicle. All because he was running three minutes behind.

Chad only listened to Compact Discs in his car because he never seemed to want to change with the times. He was obsessed with 1980s hair metal bands as well as hardcore rap. As the endless line of traffic slowly inched forward, he rolled his windows down and cranked up his stereo to Warrant's Cherry Pie. Chad sang along to the lyrics and taped his steering wheel to the drumbeat.

"She's my Cherry Pie!" he belted as he pressed in the cigarette lighter.

When it popped out, he touched the glowing orange ring to a cigarette and began to smoke. He knew smoking was probably going to cause some long-term damage, but at that moment he couldn't seem to care less.

So what, I drink too much and I smoke too much. Well, that's what an adult does after he gets a "career", he thought to himself.

He knew he made good money working for MoGo Mato Motors, but the job was beyond soul sucking. Currently, he managed a portion of their customer service call center. It currently was his job to manage twenty other daily employees. To make sure they were meeting their call requirements and not going off script on sensitive topics. If someone that worked under him had a customer who said they wanted to talk to a manager and they couldn't defuse them, he was the one they spoke with.

Some days he would do nothing but take supervisor calls. To Chad, that was the worst. Having to deal with angry customers all day long and taking their verbal abuse. Those were the times he questioned a lot of his life's decisions.

He couldn't help but notice the amount of people that looked like they were going out of town or maybe camping. Lots of people seemed to have a large amount of luggage crammed into their vehicles or strapped to the top. Normally his morning commute was filled with single drivers making their daily drudge to work. Today he was seeing entire families piled in cars, along with their kids and pets. He had to double check with himself that it was, in fact, Monday and not a holiday weekend. His cell phone confirmed that he was correct. It was Monday. It just struck him odd that there were this many people on the road coming in and out of the city like they were leaving for an extended amount of time.

Morning Fred," Chad said out his driver's side window to the security guard who worked the entrance gate for MoGo Mato Motors.

"Morning Chad. Missing coffee time, I see," the older man replied.

"Yeah, I know. Can you believe it? If I leave 5 minutes early. I'm like an hour too early, but if I leave three minutes late. I'm like twenty minutes late," Chad groaned.

"Traffic these days is a fickle bitch," Fred said as he waved him through the entrance.

Chad pulled into the lot and, to his shock, he found an open parking spot in Lot A. This was only three rows from the front door. Normally he would have to park in lot double E, which was a good quarter mile away from the entrance. Running as late as he was, he should have been stuck parking in lot double M which was more than a half mile away. So at least he had that going for him.

"Must be a lot of people out sick today," he said to himself as he got out of his car and walked into the office building.

He swiped his employee badge and entered the revolving doors of MoGo Mato Motors. There was another security guard stationed at a desk in the lobby. They both exchanged pleasantries as he walked past. He walked in, turned right, then walked about 100 steps. Chad then turned left and went down a row of gray cubicles 'til he came to his desk at the end of the row. He slid into his office chair, spun around, and turned on his computer. Thanking God that he made it to his desk unscathed. Except God didn't hear him that morning because before he could even get his computer turned on, there was Janice standing at the entrance to his workspace. Chad didn't even need to turn around because he could hear her heavy breathing.

"Good morning, Janice. What is it I can do for you?" he asked and tried to force a smile.

"Morning Bossman! Were you able to print out Friday's reports that I sent over before closing?" She asked

"No Janice, not yet. I left early Friday and I'll print them and check them over before noon," he replied.

"Okay great! Oh! Do you wanna know what happened to me on the way to work today?" she asked as Chad just smiled.

Everyone who works in a corporate job has what they call their "Arch Nemesis". Someone they just can't stand being around. Doesn't matter how hard they try, the person just rubs them the wrong way and gets under their skin. Janice was Chad's. Because of his position at work, Human Resources would seriously look down on him for telling her how he really felt. To make it even worse, Janice was constantly at his desk off and on throughout the entire day.

"Okay.. I was minding my own business, just driving along on I-35 as normal when this guy in a big pickup truck cut me off. So I was like WHOA Jack! I flipped him off and honked my horn. You know Chad, that's something I never do. That was so out of character for me," she continued.

As the lady spoke, Chad just smiled and nodded, but in his head, he hoped a lightning bolt would strike her down. Heck, he would even take the lightning bolt himself if it meant she was going to stop talking.

"After I got done honking the horn, the man slammed on his brakes and got out of the truck. Comes around to my driver's side window and starts cursing me out. Something to do with taking his daughter to the emergency room because some homeless guy bit her. He then kicked my door and told me to fuck off," Janice said anxiously.

"You should be glad that's all that happened, Janice," he said. "In today's world, someone would more than likely shoot you before discussing anything they have a problem with." This idea filled his mind with dark thoughts that made him smile.

"But he made me so angry I could just pinch someone," she said.

Go away Janice, he thought to himself as he just smiled.

"I mean, yeah, I guess you are right. He could have been packing heat and shot me," she admitted.

I could only be so lucky, Chad thought as he smiled some more.

"Say boss, what did you bring for the potluck today? I brought pink fluff," Janice said.

Chad nodded and opened his email as he ignored her question. There was an email from management stating that there were going to be a lot of people out sick today and that they still needed to hit their call volumes. He cursed under his breath. He also noticed that Janice was still standing at his desk as if waiting for something.

What do you fucking want, you annoying old goober? he thought to himself as his lips said something otherwise.

"Oh yeah? What is pink fluff?" he asked with a smile.

"Oh, it's when I take cream cheese, cottage cheese, pineapples, cherry pie filling, and cool-whip and mix it all up together into this pink fluffy desert. It's so delicious. My cats can't get enough of it," she said with a smile.

That sounds utterly horrible, he thought to himself.

"Sounds delicious can't wait. Hey do you think you could go back to your desk and jump in the queue and take some calls because we are really short-staffed today?" he asked politely.

"Sure thing, boss!" she said as she spun around and sped back to her desk.

Chad pulled up his morning reports from Friday and began checking what everyone's numbers were for last week and whether his team had met their daily requirements.

Thank you for calling MoGo Mato Motors. This is Chad. How can I help you today?" Chad said into his headset as he took the supervisor call that was forwarded by none other than Janice. The irate customer on the other end of the headset had about enough of Janice.

"You know what you can do? You can shove your company up your ass is what you can do! I was on the phone for 35 minutes with 'Janice' and she was unable to do what I asked of her," the customer spat. Chad just winced as he listened. "I told her the employees down at the dealership should all be fired. They are horrible human beings and should not be carrying the MoGo Mato Motors name and logo. I had $1.47 in change in the ashtray of my car when I brought it in for routine maintenance. When I got my car back, the money was missing!" she yelled into his earpiece.

"I am so sorry to hear that, ma'am. I do understand your frustration and I don't like to hear that any of our customers are having a bad time with our dealerships or our products," Chad said, eloquently toying with the woman's anger. "What is it exactly I could do for you today?" he asked.

"You can start by firing everyone that works in the service department. They are nothing but crooks and I think they are racists!" she spat.

Chad doodled on a pad of paper as he feigned every ounce of empathy and care he had left in his body.

"I am sorry ma'am, but the dealerships are all independently owned and are not direct employees of MoGo Mato Motors," Chad explained to the customer. While on the phone, his office room chat window dinged up on his screen.

BRO!! Did you run any dungeons last night on WoW? A message from Tyler read.

WoW was short for World of Warcraft which was an online Multi-Player Fantasy Roleplaying Game that Chad and some coworkers spent hours upon hours on when not at work.

"I am sorry ma'am I understand where you are coming from. Yes, that was very dishonest of them to do. Maybe you were mistaken, and you took the change out before you took your car to the dealer," Chad said into his headset while typing a reply to Tyler.

NO! I ended up farming for gold for like eight hours yesterday. I am getting closer to getting my legendary chest piece for my Rogue, he typed.

"Yes, ma'am, I will call and speak directly with the service manager today and let them know how you feel," he said as soon as he heard a break in her voice. He had no idea what she had just said.

NICE! You are going to love it when you get that full set of armor. Dude, did you see the news this morning? Some crazy ass shit is going on out there. Some kinda new virus seems to be spreading from overseas. Tyler's message read.

"Yes, ma'am, I will call you back later today before closing. I will let you know what the dealer has to say. Is there anything else I can help you with today? No? Thank you for calling MoGo Mato Motors, and have a lovely rest of your day. I am looking forward to speaking with you later today," Chad said, stone-faced.

No? What's happening? I was running late this morning and didn't get any coffee time. I haven't checked in with the news since Friday morning. Too busy playing WoW, Chad responded.

"Goodbye to you too, ma'am," he said as he disconnected the call. A young man named Andy popped his head over the cubicle wall in front of Chad.

"Yuck, was that one of Janice's calls?" he asked.

Chad just looked at him for a minute while he began to question the majority of his life. Would he be stuck in this soul-sucking beige penitentiary for his entire working career? Would his life have turned out better if his parents didn't move him out of the trailer park when he was seven years old away from his friends and all the things he worked so hard to achieve by then?

"Yeah…one of Janice's…I need more coffee," Chad responded and then spun his chair around and left his cubicle. He watched the computer screens switch instantly from online shopping sites to what they were supposed to be working on as he walked by.

Chad didn't care anymore what his team did. As long as they made their call numbers. That's all you have to do to survive in the corporate world. Just do the bare minimum and quietly scoot by at work, he thought. Chad had worked at MoTo Mato Motors for quite a few years now. He got the job after being laid off from a sunglass kiosk at the local mall some ten years ago. He was currently single and didn't have much of a social life. Chad was a serious introvert when it came to his personality. He wasn't really good at anything, but wasn't really bad at anything either. Just your average consumer working a white-collar job for no other reason other than a paycheck.

"Sorryyy!" Janice said as Chad walked past her cubicle.

He just ignored her and made his way to the break room. Making a note to himself that the office looked pretty decimated. There had to be more than half the usual people out today. Still, he seemed worried that he was missing some kind of holiday of some sort. Figuring he must not have been the only one, he just shrugged it off and entered the break room.

The smell of food enticed him. What few staff members were working had participated in the day's potluck lunch. The counters were lined with slow cookers and crock pots. They all contained the potluck staples such as sloppy joes, chili, tiny hot-dogs in BBQ sauce, and cheese dip. Even though Chad hated potlucks, the smells still made his mouth water. It wasn't anything against potlucks, it was just the people throwing them he usually hated. Quickly, he strolled over to the commercial coffeemaker and poured himself a fresh cup of coffee. He sighed as he realized all they had was powdered creamer and he hated powdered creamer.

"God, there's nothing worse than drinking shitty coffee with powdered creamer from a styrofoam cup," he muttered to himself.

"Hey Chad," a woman said as she glided into the room like a busybody.

"Oh hi, Sharon," he replied to the woman, then took a sip of coffee.

"What did you bring for the potluck?" she asked as she put her lunch bag into a refrigerator.

"You know me, plates and napkins like always," Chad replied with a chuckle.

Over time, he had collected a stockpile of paper plates, napkins, and plastic silverware saved up from years of potlucks. For the rest of his working career, he was pretty confident he would never actually have to bring anything to a potluck ever again.

"Oh booo, you should try to think outside the box someday and make something," Sharon said.

I probably would if I didn't hate this place and all of you in it, he thought to himself.

"Oh, you know, just not my thing. I'm cool with being the paper plate guy," he responded. They both said their goodbyes and walked back to their desks.

When Chad returned to his desk, he saw that he had 17 missed inner work messages from Tyler. Chad quickly read them all, and each one had to do with what was happening in the news. Some kind of super virus was quickly spreading across all of Europe. Millions of people were dead.

C had saw the email from HR requiring all managers to call a meeting to address global affairs. MoGo Mato Motors was going to stay open, but if anyone felt uncomfortable, they may leave. The leave, however, would be without pay and would also count against their PTO time. He sighed and bowed his head, then began typing up a mandatory meeting notice via email.

"Good morning everyone," Chad said as he walked into the meeting room and closed the door behind him. The other three managers, Lisa, Steve, and Peter, were already there.

"Listen, I know we are all worried about what's going on in the news. We called this meeting to inform you that it will be business as usual at MoGo Mato Motors. This comes from management, so don't shoot the messenger," Chad said to the room seated before him.

Everyone at a long twenty-four-foot meeting table just blinked at him.

God, I hate my job. I hate you all. Especially you, Janice, he thought to himself as he continued.

"So that brings us to… If you do not feel comfortable working here today and would like to leave to check on your families, that is okay. Just let Lisa, Steve, Peter, or myself know and we will make a note. It will not be a negative mark against you, but it will count as one of your PTO days and it will also not be a paid leave of absence," Chad said.

He winced as he heard the entire room grumble and groan.

I hope this place burns down, he thought and smiled at the idea.

"But, hey! Potluck is at noon, pretty excited for Norman's chili," he said, once again feigning his comradery.

Steve then distributed print-outs with a few scripts to say if anyone on the phone questions what's going on and what Mogo Mato Motor's stance is on the situation. It was the same rhetoric that was always sent out whenever there was a mass panic of any kind. MM Motors was owned by a Japanese company. Every year on the anniversary of Pearl Harbor, a script was handed out to phone advocates for what to say regarding the Japanese bombing. If there was an MM Motors commercial during an overly right-wing hated or overly left-wing hated TV show, the call center would hear about it. The amount of time people had on their hands always astonished Chad. The meeting room windows faced the front parking lot and the entrance gate where the security guard worked all day and every day.

Fred sat alone in his guard shack and played solitaire on his cell phone. He had worked for MM Motors since the 1990s when they first came to the United States for their base of operations in North America. He'd seen so many people come and go throughout those years. Some of which he even called friends.

Fred was a Vietnam vet who rode with the 1st Air Cavalry Division. He was active from 1965 to 1969 and even fought in the TET Offensive in 68. Fred saw a lot of action during the war and still had a hard time adjusting to normal life so many years later. His current job suited him perfectly and was a peaceful, honest living that he came to enjoy.

His game was suddenly interrupted when a panicked woman pressed herself up against the glass of his guard shack. She had long blond hair that was matted with blood and her eyes were wild with fear.

"HELP ME! YOU HAVE TO HELP ME!" the woman spat.

Fred fumbled with his phone and cursed.

"Jesus lady! What the heck is going on?" Fred inquired as he slid his window open a few inches.

"They are everywhere and they are coming this way! They look like regular people, but they aren't. My grandmother got bit by some neighborhood kid and she changed into this crazed maniac about two hours after that." The woman spoke with difficulty while panting and trying to shove her heart back into her chest.

"After that, my gram killed my grandfather and began to eat him. So I ran, and here I am. You gotta help me! I don't wanna die," she said as snot ran down her nose.

From up the road, Fred could see at least 50 people slowly shambling towards the front gate. They all looked mostly normal at first glance. It didn't take long for Fred to tell something wasn't right. The way they walked was too stiff and slow. No one walks that rigid, he thought. As they got closer, he noticed that some of them had on pajamas or just undergarments. A couple of them even looked like they were covered in blood with horrendous gaping wounds.

"About time you fuckers found me!" Fred spat as he gathered his things.

So yeah, if anyone else has any more questions? Let's wrap things up, get back to hitting those metrics and taking those calls," Chad said as his stomach turned.

An advocate named Thomas stood up from his seat and pointed out the window. "Hey, what the heck are all those people doing at Fred's shack?" he said.

Chad walked over to the window to look where the man was pointing.

"Actually, what the heck is Fred doing running across the parking lot with that woman?" another advocate said.

They all noticed Fred running wildly across the lot with a strange woman behind him. They made it to the front revolving door, and he slid his card through the reader to make the door slowly spin and let them in.

"Lisa, could you please call security and have them go check out the front gate and see what's going on?" Chad said.

Lisa leaned over the conference table to the hands-free phone that sat in the center and pressed the number for security.

"Alright everyone, let's get back to work. Those phones won't answer themselves. You have 5 minutes to get back to your desk and get situated before Peter here turns the queue back on," Chad said.

After wrangling everyone out of the conference room and back to their desks, he disappeared into the bathroom and entered a stall where he sat down to collect his thoughts and be alone. Was there some serious stuff happening? Something he didn't know about? Was this so-called virus as bad as they said? Should he say fuck this place and just go home? Chad started to worry that all the people he saw on the way to work who looked like they were leaving were actually leaving. He now felt that they all knew more than he knew about what was going on. When he left the bathroom, he heard the first calls start to come in and the workplace went back to normal.

Chad sat back down at his desk and pulled up his email to see if management had any other information coming down the pipeline. He saw an email notification pop up, so he clicked on it. It just so happened that it was from headquarters back in Japan. The email stated that the corporate offices in Japan would no longer be available today and have been sent home due to the current global situation. It then went on to explain that they expect all other branches to remain working as usual. Furthermore, it went on to instruct them to be empathetic to anyone that wants to leave for the day. However, that will be on their dime and the company will not pay for the time off. Chad just shook his head and saved the e-mail, just in case he needed it someday.

L ooks like we got a pickle of a situation, Stew," Fred said to the guard at the front desk. He then helped the younger woman to a chair so she could sit for a minute and catch her breath. Stewart stepped from behind the front desk and walked over to stand next to Fred. They both looked through the glass doors that framed the front of the entrance to MM Motors. There was now a sea of people slowly making their way across the parking lot to the building's entrance.

"I'd say a pickle would be an understatement," Fred said while looking across the lot in awe.

As the people got closer, their features came into view. Most of them were covered in gore and some were even missing arms or even a leg in some cases. They just kinda haphazardly shuffled or dragged themselves across the pavement. Some even leave a trail of guts across the concrete.

"Don't exactly seem to be in much of a hurry, do they?" the woman asked.

"God damn zombies, Stew," Fred replied to both with a stern look.

C had came down to the main lobby to see what all the commotion was about. The call queue was currently down and it seemed the phones in general were no longer working. Members of his team were starting to get nervous because no one could contact the outside world by phone.

Before heading down to the main lobby area, Chad checked his iPhone and saw that he had no service either. This wasn't much of an alarm to him because dead zones happened all the time in their building. It was always horrible to do anything on your cell phone while at work. When Chad walked into the foyer, he couldn't believe what he was seeing.

There were about thirteen people total in the lobby, which included five security guards, a strange woman, and six other managers from each floor of MM Motors. A couple of them all dropped their coffee mugs at the same time when they saw what was pressing against the front doors and windows. The walking dead were lined up across the front entrance of the building.

"Holy shit," Chad said. As he sipped heavily on his coffee.

"Jesus Christ…What the hell are they?" one of the other managers asked in an emotionless daze.

Another manager vomited on the floor.

"See Stew… fuckin Zombies," Fred said, poking his right finger at the glass while speaking to Stewart.

Stewart put his face close to the window. Examining the old lady in curlers who seemed to be lifelessly staring at him. It was like she was chewing at the air in front of her.

Undead from all walks of life pressed against the glass now. Some looked like normal people who varied in age, with glassy milky eyes and a gaping mouth. Others, however, had various forms of lesions or trauma. A little girl in a Hello Kitty onesie was missing her right arm. An elderly lady in her late 80s was missing a jaw and an eyeball. They all clawed and scraped at the glass barrier between them and the people inside. The sounds of moans and squeaking glass made it hard for them to think straight.

"Ran into a few of these sumbitches in Nam," Fred said while tapping on the glass. He furrowed his brow at Stewart.

"What did you do?" someone asked.

"Head-shots. The only way to kill 'em. Well, besides blowing them up or burning them to ash," Fred said.

Stewart just responded by standing there with his mouth open.

"Okay, Stewart, I want you to check with management on how they want us to handle this," Chad said as he took charge of the situation.

"For now, let's just not let any of them inside. I'll email management when I get back to my desk and CC you all on it. Let's see what they want us to do about the current situation. Just stay clear of the doors and we will go from there," Chad said, then he turned around and began to walk back to his desk.

When Chad got back to his desk, he noticed everyone was staring at him as he walked. The entire department was completely silent as they seemed to wait for him to say something. Chad sighed heavily.

"Okay, everyone… everything is okay. I am going to send an email to management and see what they want us to do about all this… and we are going to go from there," Chad motioned with his hands up, as he tried to calm them all. When he finally got to his desk, he noticed he had a message from Tyler.

DUDE!!!!!!!!!!!!!!!!!!!!!! WTF is going on!!!!!!! Tyler's message read.

Ugh, I have no idea dude. Now I gotta email Management and ask WTF are we supposed to do now? Chad's response read.

The MM Motors building was an older building that was built back in the 1980s and still had its phone and internet run through separate lines. So even though their phones were down and there was no cell-phone reception, they were able to still have limited access to the web. Chad figured the system was just bogged down due to whatever was going on in the outside world. He took another long, heavy drink of coffee before he started his email to management.

F red and Stewart entered the custodian closet to see what they could find that would work as makeshift weapons. Stewart had emailed management, and they told him to call the police and keep it business as usual. Stewart didn't bother to tell them he had no way of calling the police because by now he didn't see the point. So they were basically on their own now.

"If that many are out there now, Stew. That means there's a lot more of them all over town. Their bite spreads fast. Within two hours, you're infected," Fred said as he handed Stewart a mop.

Stewart just looked at the mop, then back to Fred.

"Trust me, we can use that if those fuckers get in… and I think they will," Fred said to Stewart as he picked up his own mop. He began to unscrew the mop head from its handle. Then he retrieved a roll of duct tape and a medium-sized Phillips screwdriver. Fred then began to unroll the duct tape and tape the screwdriver to his mop handle.

"See here. Now we have a spear. All it takes is a quick tap to the head and they go down like a sack of potatoes," Fred said with confidence.

Stewart began to do the same thing to his mop.

"Hey guys, is there anything I can do to help? I feel kinda odd just sitting in the lobby staring at what I think is my dead grandmother," the woman said to the two men fabricating medieval weaponry from a janitor's closet.

"What's your name, ma'am?" Fred asked.

"Alice," she quickly responded.

"Whelp, you can grab what you can from here and turn it into whatever you can to keep you from dying," Fred said without beating around the bush.

Alice nodded and quickly grabbed up a push broom and began to unscrew the brush.

Jesus Christ dude..... Just heard back from management. They want us to sit tight and wait for the phones to come back up. Apparently, someone from I.T. is working on fixing the issue. Until then, everyone is to do busy work until we know more. Chad's message read to Tyler.

Janice popped around the corner of his cubicle office with her usual smile as he hit send.

"Can I help you, Janice?" Chad said without a smile.

"Hey. Any word from management yet?" she asked.

"Yeah, I'm sending out an email blast right now to everyone," Chad said as he typed away at his keyboard furiously.

Janice just stood there waiting for him to say or do something else.

"Go back to your desk, Janice," Chad said and pointed in her direction.

Janice pouted and turned and walked back to her cubicle that, of course, was covered with cat photos and motivational sayings.

DUDE! THIS TOTALLY SUCKS ASS! Tyler's message read.

No kidding. I knew I should have just stayed in bed this morning and not come in. Chad responded.

It had been about three hours since Chad emailed the team to let them know to just keep working on their caseloads and notes. His email emphasized using the time wisely to the best of their ability. He was quite surprised at the lack of backlash he received from the staff. They seriously couldn't go anywhere because that would require going out one of the many doors that were now covered with undead trying to get in. Just shortly after Chad sent his email to his floor, the internet went down completely. They still had power, but many of them questioned how long that would be. Chad sipped once more at his coffee as he walked down his row of cubicles.

"Hey Chad, how long do you think we will be working till today?" Martin asked as Chad walked past.

"Full day, Martin. Business as usual until told otherwise," Chad responded without stopping.

He was starting to get annoyed at all the questions. He thought his email was crystal clear. In a nutshell, he told everyone to stay at their desks and shut up. Most days, he wished that's the exact verbiage he could use, but Human Resources would not take kindly to that.

When Chad entered the lobby to see how things were progressing, he quickly realized things had gotten much worse. The glass surrounding the revolving door of the lobby entrance was now smeared with blood and bile that cast the lobby with a yellowish-brown tint. The number of presumed undead outside had now tripled. Fred, Stewart, and Alice had moved all the lobby furniture against the entrance to form a blockade. They even wedged a few things into the revolving doors. He could see the silhouettes of the dead rocking side to side as they pressed up against the windows, trying to get at the living now trapped inside.

"Jesus Christ!" Chad spat.

Standing in front of him were Fred, Stewart, and Alice, all holding makeshift weapons from the janitor's closet. Each weapon resembled a polearm or spear that had been fabricated from mop or broom handles with whatever they could find to make a sharp edge or point. With a little duct tape and imagination, they were good to go.

"What the fuck is going on? Stewart, what did management tell you?" he asked.

"They told him it was business as usual and to call the cops and let them deal with it. He was told that under no circumstances should he go out and engage these people," Fred said, barging in before Stewart could open his mouth to speak.

"The cops are not coming. I had to run a good two miles before I got to Fred and all hell had already broken loose. Everywhere… from what I could see," Alice said, interrupting the three men.

"I'm sorry, and who are you?" Chad asked, annoyed.

"Sorry, my name is Alice. My grandma ate my grandpa, and she's now standing just outside those doors," she said as she pointed to the gore smeared entrance.

"I'm sorry for your loss, Alice," Chad said.

The moans and thuds from the creatures outside got louder once Chad began speaking to whom he now called the "Three Musketeers".

"So we have no way of getting through to management because the internet is down. So, should we treat this as a tornado drill?" Chad asked.

Fred and Stewart just looked at each other, then back at Chad.

"Let me see your Security Operations binder, Stewart. There has to be something in there that can give us an idea of what to do in a situation like this," Chad said as he walked around the front security counter. Quickly, he located the ten-pound binder with color-coded tabs along the edges. He dropped it to the desk with a thud. He thumbed through the tabs until he came to a section titled Emergency Procedures. The moaning from beyond the glass barrier continued to increase in volume.

"Let's see, it's not a fire drill… Ha! Can't do that now, can we?" Chad said with a chuckle.

The other three just looked at each other and back at Chad. They all simultaneously wondered why this man was looking through a binder to figure out how to live or die.

"Okay, tornado drill. That's not what I'm looking for," Chad said as he continued to thumb through the pages. Pausing every once in a while to take a sip from his coffee.

"Wow, there is actually a tab for terrorist attacks. And it says to evacuate the building immediately. Can't do either, can we?" Chad said as he laughed.

"Is there access to the roof?" Alice asked. Seeing how none of the men were taking charge.

"Yes! Yes, there is," Fred said with excitement.

Chad paused from his binder and raised an eyebrow at the conversation unfolding in front of him. The dead outside were still growing in numbers as the glass began to make an audible creak from the weight.

"That's a great idea, Alice. We can hopefully signal someone to rescue us," Fred said.

As the three of them were about to leave. The security alarm began to wail in an increasingly high-pitched squeal.

"That's one of the side doors! Someone must have come in or out without their badge," Fred said.

They all ran towards where Fred thought it was coming from. Chad just closed the binder and watched them all runoff.

Of course... What now… Chad thought to himself. After taking another deep drink from his coffee cup, he figured he might as well go see what was going on.

The Three Musketeers ran past the break room as the advocates inside set up the afternoon potluck. Others on the floor began to stand up from their cubicles to see what all the commotion was about.

"Where the heck is the rest of security?" Fred spat into his radio.

As they turned the corridor on the far west end of the building, they saw where the other security officers were. They stopped ten yards from the door and stood there a minute to take in the sight of what was unfolding in front of them. They found the rest of security sprawled out before them in a pile of gore and entrails. Alice winced and tried to keep the contents of her stomach where they were for the time being.

"It's just like 'Nam again," Fred said to anyone who was listening.

Before them lay the five remaining guards. On top of them were the dead. They were ripping and tearing away chunks of flesh and hungrily shoveling it into their mouths. A total of six of them were inside the MM Motors building and one seemed to be stuck halfway through the door as it tried to close itself.

Even though the door alarm was still screeching, the three of them could still hear the wet munching and chewing from just a few feet away. Fred nodded to Stewart and Alice, then made his way to the closest infected and jammed it in the temple with his homemade spear. The zombie fell motionless to the ground as soon as Fred's spear hit what was left of the thing's brain.

"See. Go for the head. Yeah, gotta scramble a zombie's brains to kill 'em for good!" Fred yelled over the door alarm. Then he turned and repeated the process on the next closest one. Alice and Stewart followed Fred's lead and began dispatching the rest.

"What do we do with this one?" Alice yelled to the others as she pointed to the one that was wedged in the side exit door, half in and half out.

Fred quickly jabbed the zombie granny in the temple and Alice used her foot to push the body out the door, causing it to slam. Once it closed, the alarm finally shut off. Victorious, they looked around to take in the glory of a job well executed. The entire west end of the 1st floor was standing in the hallway staring at them. All of them seemed extremely unnerved.

That's when Chad lost it.

"What the actual fuck is going on?" Chad spat while still holding his coffee cup, as the dead moaned and thudded against the door to the outside.

"He seems nice," Alice whispered sarcastically to Stewart.

"What the actual fuck! Alice, you're not even cleared to be in here! What... the hell… just fucking happened!" Chad yelled hysterically. He didn't notice the light pressure that was slowly clamping around his right ankle. Without spilling a drop of coffee, Chad continued to yell at everyone.

"You know what? I am trying very hard right now to not lose my shit on all of you," Chad said, as his temper continued to boil to the point of explosion.

The Three Musketeers were standing in front of him, gruesomely covered in human gore and out of breath. They looked like some horror movie rejects from a Sam Raimi film. Behind Chad stood the majority of the first floors work staff. Some of them were eating from paper plates as they tried to figure out what all the commotion was about.

Everyone was currently staring at Chad.

"That's it! That's fucking it! I've had it. All of you can just go to hell. Especially you Janice! You know what? Fuck you, Janice," Chad spat as he pointed at the older lady, who just looked confused and lost.

"Yeah, you all heard me. I quit! I can't… and never could stand any of you! Not you Sharon. Not you Lisa. Not even you, Walter," Chad said as he pointed his finger at them.

While everyone was distracted, the security guard who had recently been partially eaten took a chunk out of Chad's right ankle. He screamed in pain as he tried to kick the security guard off his right foot.

"I thought you said it took your grandma two hours to turn?" Fred whispered to Alice as they watched Chad dance around and panic as the guard tried to eat more of his leg.

"My grandma was bitten while she was alive. That guy there was dead. So I guess you turn faster if you get bit and die?" Alice said with a small amount of confidence.

Chad was now flailing his arms around in panic as everyone just watched. They all seemed unsure of what exactly they were looking at.

Stewart stepped forward and drove his trusty mop-spear into the fresh zombies' temple, and it instantly stopped moving. Chad turned and pushed his way through the crowd of co-workers and limped his way back to his desk. The rest of the crowd turned around back to look for direction from the Three Musketeers. That's when the remaining four security guards began to stand up. Everyone screamed and ran in the opposite direction.

"This can't be good," Alice said.

The four security guards opened their maws and let out moans of hunger as they tried to shamble their way toward anything that had a pulse.

C had sat at his desk and pulled off his right shoe and sock to inspect his wound. The entire floor had panicked and ran in all directions. He couldn't care less. Ten years he worked there. Gave up a lot of his time to go the extra mile and build a career. Do all the things they program you to do as you grow up. Go to school, go to college, then get your degree. After that you get a day job, pay taxes, and work til you die.

As Chad sat and blotted at his bite wound with a Christmas-themed cocktail napkin, he realized that he had not taken a vacation in those entire ten years of working at MoGo Mato Motors. All he did was work and play video games. He worked all the overtime he could and even worked all the holidays with no problem. The point was to advance his way up in the company.

Chad had done pretty well over the last ten years, but what did Chad have to show for it? A mountain of debt, depression, and disillusion. That's what he accumulated at MM Motors.

"God damn it!" Chad spat as he looked at the bite on his foot. It looked even worse than it did when he first sat down.

"God damn it! Ten FUCKING years in this shit hole and I get a zombie bite on the fucking job!" he yelled as he began to type his letter of resignation.

The first floor was complete pandemonium. Nobody knew what to do. Some employees ran back to their desks and pretended to keep working. Others quickly grabbed their slow cookers and crock pots from the break room and ran back to their desks to gather their things. Those who tried to leave ran to the lobby entrance. They all quickly saw just how bad things actually were. There were now hundreds of zombies pressed against the front doors and windows. The rotating door vibrated from the strain of the bodies pressing against it as they tried to get at those inside. A few people screamed in horror. Meanwhile, the rest of the first floor's occupants looked at the old war vet for some kind of leadership.

"Okay, let's try to stay calm," Fred belted as he tried to corral those who still might have their wits.

The Three Musketeers had taken down the remaining four guards before anyone managed to find themselves bitten. Stewart and Alice helped Fred up onto the closest desk so people could hear him better. For the first time, Stew realized how old Fred was.

"I'm pretty sure most of you know who I am. So I'll be brief. What we have here are zombies. Yup, the real deal, walking dead, shoot 'em in the head zombies. From what we can tell so far is that these bastards are slow. Just like the ones I fought in Vietnam," Fred said as his eyes grew wilder.

About 25 office workers were standing around listening to him.

"We've decided that our safest place right now is the roof. All of us should make our way up the stairs from here. We will stop on every floor and see who we can gather up. Hopefully, when someone comes to rescue us, and I am sure they will, they will see us from the top of the building," Fred spoke as if he was giving a speech from a George C. Scott movie.

Everyone listening seemed to look at each other and nod in agreement. It sounded like the best option. All the windows were now swarming with walking dead trying to get in, and they were at all the entrances and exits. There currently was no way in or out.

Fred, Alice, and Stewart gathered together in the stairwell of the 4th floor. Behind them was a rag-tag army of customer care advocates from the 2nd and 3rd floors. It had taken them about an hour and a half to run through both floors and gather up who was willing to follow them to the roof. There were now about forty-five of them total and all of them were armed with homemade weapons from the janitor and supply closets on each floor.

"We ain't pretty, but goddamnit, we got guts," Fred said to his team as they huddled together in the stairwell.

Janice was in front of the group, holding a claw hammer in each hand. The 62-year-old woman's mascara and eyeliner ran down her cheeks like Viking war paint. This impressed Fred. He figured she would be the first to go, but for some reason the old girl had spunk.

"Okay, everyone. Fred says we have two more floors till we get to the roof access," Alice said to the white-collar militia in front of her. Even though she was a complete stranger to all of these people, they seemed to respond to her confidence. Before today, Alice was just a bank manager at one of the branch offices in downtown Austin. She didn't have any kids or siblings, and her parents died when she was a teenager. Her grandparents raised her and up until this morning, they were alive and well. Now she worried her gram gram was wandering the halls of MoGo Mato Motors in search of someone to eat and, more than likely, had found someone.

They cleared the 2nd and 3rd floors pretty quickly and without much trouble. Some of the people that worked on that floor decided to go with them and others decided to take their chances with whatever was going on outside and get back to their families.

Alice knew that those who decided to leave wouldn't get very far because no one was getting through the front entrance alive in its current state. The MoGo Mato Motors building was a weapons-free zone that also included security guards as well. The situation probably would have gone a little better if the security force at MM Motors wasn't just armed with pepper spray. They were all trained to subdue and contain. The procedure was to wait for the authorities to arrive and handle the rest. That training didn't do them any good, seeing how the 73-year-old man the company put out to pasture in the front guard shack was one of the last ones standing.

"Okay people, is everyone ready?" Fred shouted as he raised his mop spear. Before anyone could chime in, the power to the building went out, and for ten long seconds, they all stood in the dark before the red emergency lights came on.

"Aww pickle-shoes!" Fred spat.

The group stood silent and didn't make a move.

"Okay, there should still be daylight coming into the windows on the 4th and 5th floors. Plus, the emergency lights have kicked on," Alice said.

Fred nodded and kicked open the door with his left foot. The Three Musketeers rushed through the door triumphantly and came to a complete halt. All of them seemed to gasp at once at what they saw.

"Okay… this isn't good," Fred said as he took it all in.

The linoleum floor in front of them was smeared with fresh blood and viscera. Cubicle walls were knocked over and the entire 4th floor looked like a category three tornado had run rampant. The main aisle that ran from east to west was covered in half-eaten bodies and paperwork. Some of them had already become infected and were starting to crawl their way towards Fred and his crew. The screams of those who still remained alive could be heard echoing across the office space.

"We have to help them," Alice said, as she pointed to the opposite end of the floor.

Stewart nodded in agreement.

"This floor holds about 250 people. Even if half that many are infected and have turned, we are majorly fubared," Fred responded.

Janice stepped forward.

"From what I heard this morning from my friend Kate, there were only like 50 people total that came in today on this floor. I say we can handle that. There are about 45 of us here now. Plus, these things are super slow and, by my guess, are not very bright," she said and pointed to one that was slowly crawling their way.

The top half of a middle-aged woman in a business suit dragged herself through the entrails of her fellow workers. Like a wet rag mop leaving a trail of fresh blood behind it.

Carefully trying not to slip on the wet floor, Stewart made his way towards the crawling woman. He pulled out a large flathead screwdriver as he knelt beside her. She was snapping her jaws together as she tried to bite at him while he held her head to the floor. Stewart took the screwdriver and slowly drove it through the woman's left ear canal and, with a wet pop, she ceased moving and fell limp. Stewart looked back at Janice and Fred as he gave a thumbs-up while smiling.

"Whelp Janice. I guess that's our answer. Any of you that don't think they can cut the mustard are free to go back the way we came or hang tight here 'til we call for you," Fred ordered. The group took a second and looked at each other and then back at Fred. No one moved. This brought a tear to Fred's eye as he nodded with pride.

"Alright, people. Watch our flanks and those in the back watch our six. I was in worse situations on the Ho Chi Minh Trail back in 68. I've dealt with these Zed Heads before with less and made it out alive. Staying together means staying alive. We can do this!" Fred spat as the crowd cheered.

Chad had managed to limp himself to the elevator and take it up to the 5th floor before the power went out. He wanted to get a look from the break room. The 5th floor had the best view and you could even see a little of Austin's skyline. Chad always wished he worked on this floor, but this was reserved for all the American higher-ups in MoGo Mato Motor management. He thought it was odd that everyone on this floor did not come in today. They all were working from home. This led him to believe that maybe that was on purpose. Maybe management knew what was happening or at least had a heads-up of what was coming. He shook his head at the thought of those with money living better lives in today's economy. Lives that were better than those that actually made the world work through blood, sweat, and tears.

"Economy," Chad chuckled as he began to cough violently.

His entire body was beginning to hurt to the touch. The joints in his knees and elbows felt stiff and painful as if he was in his 90s. His jaw dropped at the sight of how lavish the break room on the 5th floor was. Windows ran the entire north side of the room, providing a view of the surrounding landscape and treetops. The room had hardwood flooring and soft, overstuffed coaches to sit on.

There was a fully stocked bar on the far left wall from where he was standing. There were even stools for people to sit on while they ordered whatever they wanted. On the other side of the room were various massage chairs for people to sit in on their breaks and have a masseuse take care of them.

"You have to be shitting me," Chad said to himself as he hobbled over to the bar.

From behind the bar, he reached up to the top shelf and pulled down a bottle of MacCallan 18-year-old scotch. He took a glass from underneath and poured himself a healthy five finger pour. Gently, he swirled the brown liquid in front of his face before he took in the deep smells of fine oak barrels, spices, and a hint of vanilla. He took a long sip and closed his eyes for a split second.

"Well, I'll be damned. It is that good," Chad said to himself, then took another drink.

A large mirror ran the length of the entire bar, which caused him to pause and examine his current situation.

"Jesus, I look awful," he said while noticing how gaunt his face had become over the last hour and a half. The whites of his eyes had become an off shade of yellow and his cheeks were now sunken in.

I'm so hungry, maybe I should eat something? He thought to himself.

Nursing his right foot, he limped across the break room with his glass of scotch and opened the commercial-sized refrigerator. There wasn't anything to eat in the fridge, but Chad did notice there were two unopened half gallons of half-and-half creamer. This sent him over the edge. He took one of the half gallons in his right hand and whipped it at the window in a rage.

"Those motherfuckers!" he screamed as he watched the white cream trickle down the glass and onto the clean wooden floor.

So you've dealt with zombies before?" Alice asked Fred while she kicked a corpse to see if it would move. "I am really surprised at how calm I am…now knowing now they exist." Alice drove her mop handle through a dead man's head as it tried to bite her tennis shoe. A squirt of blood shot past both of their faces as she twisted the handle in mid-conversation.

"Afraid so. There was a nasty mess of them down a North Vietnamese tunnel system back in 1969. We always figured it was the Russians who came up with it. Those communist bastards would do anything to win," Fred said as he wrinkled his brow.

The group began to approach the conference room at the east end of the floor. The cries for help had gotten louder the closer they got. Unfortunately, so did the moans of the dead. The group stopped and hid behind a line of cubicle walls to regroup.

"How many Zed Heads do you count?" Fred whispered as he seemed to wheeze and catch his breath.

Alice could tell the old man was in great shape, but they had already taken down ten zombies and climbed two flights of stairs in the last two hours. She was in her 30s and considered herself in great shape and was exhausted. She couldn't imagine what the old man was going through.

"I think I counted 24 of them. All swarming around the door and windows of that meeting room," Alice responded.

Stewart nodded in agreement to her answer. So far, they hadn't lost anyone from their group. Everyone seemed to be holding their own, but then again, the Three Musketeers had done all the heavy lifting up until now.

"Okay, I like those odds," Fred said to the group.

"There are more of us than them. I think if we pair up and take 'em out two on one we can do this," Alice whispered.

Stewart gave a thumbs up as a few others nodded.

"I'll go with Stew," Janice said as the others began to pair off.

"Alright everyone, ready?" Fred whispered.

"Let's do this!" Alice spat.

"For RIVENDELL!" Janice suddenly screamed as the group charged. Fred and Alice held up their hands to stop everyone from charging at once.

"Wait. WAIT!" Fred screamed as he tried to get everyone's attention, but he was too late. The group had already entered the melee.

To Fred's surprise, it went way worse than he hoped.

C had had managed to slide one of the couches over in front of the wall of glass that ran the length of the room. There he sat with his bottle of 18-year-old scotch and watched the outside world burn. He could no longer stand. He was so weak, and it had become harder to breathe.

Pillars of smoke reached for the heavens across the horizon. Over towards Austin, it looked worse. He just smiled cynically as he sipped his scotch.

"I did everything I was supposed to do in life," he mumbled.

Three A-10 Warthogs roared past in the sky, causing the windows to vibrate.

"Graduated high school with decent grades. Went to a university after that. Got me a bachelor's of business and began to climb the corporate ladder," he said to nobody as he took another drink, then topped off his glass.

Six military Black Hawk helicopters flew by overhead and fanned out over the treetops. A couple of them hovered in certain areas as they launched rockets and fired their chain guns at whatever was on the ground below them.

"Bought myself a home by the time I was 26, in fucking Austin. Worked my ass off, taking as much overtime as I could. Ruined my social life in the process," he said.

A massive ball of fire rose from Austin's skyline from far off. Chad now began to cough up blood. The bite wound on his right ankle now looked severely infected and was oozing with puss.

"These fuckers knew something was happening. They had to have. They could have at least sent out a memo." The rocks glass crashed to the floor as Chad toppled over in agony. He clenched at his stomach as he tried to howl out in pain, but no sounds came out of his mouth any-more…

Janice swung her hammers with such grace she resembled a symphony conductor. Her business casual attire was now soaked in blood, and her eyes were full of fury. She struck one zombie in the head after another. Their offensive didn't exactly go according to plan. There wasn't a plan.

After Fred's speech, the group ran into battle before he could even explain his plan. Between the lack of organization and failure to cooperate, the group fell apart as soon as the living dead turned their attention to them. Most of them tripped over each other. Since the floor was covered in blood, it was all just an utter clusterfuck. A few of them froze at the sight of coworkers who were missing parts of their faces or limbs.

This hesitation started a chain reaction of death. As slow and brainless as the zombies are, they were utterly relentless. Once one person fell or froze up, that was all the time that was needed for one to shamble over and latch its jaws around someone's arm, shoulder, or hand. One advocate swung blindly only to strike her partner in the back of the head, sending them unconsciously head over heels into two zombies and ultimately a gruesome death.

"Jesus, this is like watching a one-legged cat try to bury a turtle in a frozen pond," Fred said as he winced. He stood there, not moving, as he watched it all unfold in front of him. Out of the 45 survivors they gathered, only Fred, Janice, Alice, and Stewart remained. Out of the 24 zombies they had to get through to help the people trapped in the conference room, 28 now remained.

"How the fuck did we end up with more than we started?" Alice spat as she knocked over two with her mop handle.

The ones in the group that died were reanimated quicker than they had hoped.

"We can't win this," Fred said as he stabbed an overweight man in a Hawaiian shirt in the eye socket.

"I say we run and head straight for the roof. Hopefully, these guys try to follow us, and that allows those people a chance to run…" Alice paused.

In all the commotion, they didn't pay attention to the people trapped in the conference room behind the wall of advancing dead. Someone among them had been infected before holing up. That person must have turned and if those people fought anything like their coworkers, they were doomed before the fight even started. The screams for help had stopped and now all they heard were the moans of the dead echoing through the office.

"This was a colossal waste of time and we are beyond FUBAR now," Fred spat. The old man was visibly beginning to tire. He was having a hard time holding the advancing dead off him.

"Guys! Screw this! There's a stairwell over there. I say we make a break for it and head straight to the roof," Alice yelled over the moans.

Janice buried one of her claw hammers into a man's skull, then wrenched it free.

"That was Albert. I liked Albert. We were in a book club together for the past five years," Janice said regretfully, while bringing her other hammer down on another man's head.

"That was Matt. He was a dick," she said as Matt's body dropped to the floor.

"Alice is right. The hell with this!" Fred yelled. The four remaining survivors bolted for the east end stairwell.

The thing that had once been Chad opened its milky white eyes and stood up. It looked around the breakroom as if it had never been there before.

It would take another year for what was left of the scientific community to learn about the virus. How it affected those people with the rare blood type AB Negative differently. Only about one percent of the world's population carries this blood type. The majority of the population, once infected, turned into a brainless carcass of what they once were. Their only drive was to eat the meat of the living. They were slow, uncoordinated, and lacked any cognitive brain activity. Some scientists believed that the virus was trying to spread and survive, while others thought it was an act of God. Those with AB-negative blood, however, were changed into something completely different.

Something in this blood type would turn a person into what would be later known as a "screamer". These were a faster, more barbaric breed of the undead. They were cunning, fast, and much more lethal than their slower counterparts. They could navigate simple tasks like opening doors and climbing stairs. These "screamers" also had a very acute sense of smell. This allowed them to track and sniff out groups of survivors for miles.

Chad just so happened to be AB Negative.

Fred pointed up towards the ceiling of the east stairwell to a small hatch. In the corner was a steel ladder that led up towards their perceived salvation.

"Okay… I'm gonna climb the ladder and open the hatch and check things out first," Fred whispered.

Just over his left shoulder, Alice noticed something in the small window of the door marked "5th Floor".

Chad? she thought. Then she snapped out of her daze.

"Are you sure you can climb all the way up there?" Alice asked the old army veteran.

"Yeah, I think I can if I go slow and be careful. It shouldn't be a problem," Fred said.

They could hear the hungry moans of the dead from the landing below them.

"Look! Zombies can't climb stairs," Janice said. She pointed down towards the group of coworkers that just stood there reaching upwards towards a meal they could not obtain.

"They must have pushed the door open somehow," Alice said.

"I thought they couldn't open doors?" Janice asked.

"They can't. They must have gotten lucky and the weight of them got the door to swing open," Fred said.

"Okay, we should probably hurry this along before they manage to do something else," Alice said.

"Okay, Alice is right. None of us are getting any younger," Fred said as he readied himself to climb. He took a deep breath and placed his hands on a rung just above his head.

The door to the 5th floor behind them slowly creaked open. In the doorway stood the thing that was once named Chad. The northeastern regional manager of MoGo Mato Motors Customer Care Center stood there looking at them. He no longer resembled the man he once was. His eyes had turned milky white, and his skin had become jaundiced. Purple veins spider webbed across his gaunt face and exposed skin.

"Aw... shitbirds," Fred said.

The others stood speechless in the presence of this new threat. Without warning, it rushed at them, giving off an ear-piercing scream.

Stewart and Alice were knocked aside as it latched onto Fred. The old Vietnam veteran tried his best to wrestle this new super-zombie off him. He just didn't have anything left in the tank and was overcome with ease. Arterial spray shot out of the man's neck as the thing that was once Chad sunk its teeth into his soft skin.

The two fell to the floor as the thing began to pull chunks out of Fred's neck and shoulder.

"You motherfucker!" Janice cried at the top of her lungs. She fearlessly charged, bringing her claw hammer down towards Chad's head.

She missed.

The full force of her blow went into Fred's forehead, killing him instantly.

"Go! Go! Go!" Alice screamed while pushing Stewart towards the ladder.

"Oh, no. Oh no," Janice said in regret. She dropped the hammer as she looked in shock and horror at what she had done. She couldn't register that Fred was already doomed, and she did him a favor.

With a screech, Chad shot up from Fred's corpse and lunged at Janice. She tried to block his charge with her forearms, to no avail. Chad's momentum pushed them both back into the railing as his teeth clamped down on the meat of her left forearm.

Janice's reaction time was perfect. She grabbed Chad and rolled herself backward. Using Chad's force and momentum to her favor in one last, valiant effort, they both flipped over the railing and toppled down the stairwell. They ping-ponged off the railings on each floor as they plunged. Like two limp rag dolls, they hit the ground level with a wet splat. Janice was already dead before she hit the floor, having broken her neck on the way down. Chad's head cracked open like a mush-melon as all 215 pounds of him landed head first on the tile floor.

S tewart flipped the hatch to the roof open and helped Alice out of the small hole. They both stood there a minute and let the warmth of the sun bring them a few seconds of peace. That was short-lived once they looked around the surrounding landscapes.

As far as they could see, everything looked like utter chaos. Black smoke clouds billowed up from the tree lines in all directions. Off in the distance, the city of Austin smoldered. The sounds of sirens, explosions, and gunfire echoed through the air. It was chaos.

"Holy shit," Alice said.

Stewart just shook his head in disbelief at what would later be known as "The Day The World Ended".

"I guess we wait up here and hopefully a rescue chopper will eventually fly over. I hope," Alice said in a half question, half statement.

Stewart just shrugged, indicating that he had no clue what to do next.

"I say we give it a couple of hours. After that, maybe we should try to go back down and look for some keys and a car?" she asked. Stewart pointed down towards the lobby entrance of the building. Alice gasped at the sight below.

The horde of dead had made its way through the front windows. The screams of those trapped inside could be heard up on the roof.

"Oh my God, those poor people. What were they doing there? Why didn't they at least head to another level? They would have been safer on the second floor." Alice said with empathy.

Stewart just shook his head.

Their screams didn't last very long. The two of them stood in silence as they watched the carnage below. The horde now numbered in the thousands. There was no way the two of them would be able to make it safely to any of the vehicles in the parking lot.

The remaining Two Musketeers sat on the roof for another three hours as the numbers below kept increasing. Just when they began to lose hope, the thumping noise of a helicopter broke their silence.

A Sikorsky S-76 air ambulance approached them from the north.

Alice peered out the window of the S-76 as they flew away from MoGo Mato Motors. The chaos and carnage below was overwhelming. Homes were on fire, bodies lay in the streets, and masses of the dead were everywhere. She quickly realized that they would not have gotten very far if they had tried to leave by car. She reassured herself that they made the right decision. "Fred" made the right decision and she was grateful to have met him.

"Hey Stewart," she said as she leaned over towards a man that as of yesterday she didn't even know existed.

He looked over at her with curiosity.

"What does Fubar mean?" she asked as she tried to speak over the sound of the helicopter.

"Fucked Up Beyond All Recognition," Stewart replied.

EPILOGUE:

Greg took his time clearing the floors of MoGo Mato Motors. He made sure every inch of the building was empty before he was distracted by searching for keys or supplies. The lobby and the 4th floor had been hit the worst and were littered with long-dead casualties. It was hard to tell with the level of decomposition who was who, but he made sure everything in the building was, in fact, dead. The 2nd and 3rd floors looked like a time capsule of a world now long lost and forgotten.

Greg never really understood the appeal of a corporate job and never thought it was for him. The thought of being trapped inside a building for eight hours or more a day and stuck in a cubicle always made his skin crawl. Trapped by golden handcuffs, the promise of material success, and addicted to what was expected. This left you a shell of a person who might as well be dead.

Greg planned to clear his way to the 5th floor, then begin his search and work his way back down. He made sure to go slow and allow time for George to catch up and know where he was at all times. Stopping to take a deep breath, he readied himself for the worst before opening the east door to the fifth floor. As soon as the door was open enough, the calico shot ahead of Greg and pranced ahead at his leisure.

"You do you, George," Greg called out after the cat, which just ignored him.

"Wow. Look at this place," he said as he looked around.

Unlike the other floors, this one did not have a floor plan that was filled with cubicles, cheap office carpet, and linoleum. The north and south sides of the floor were lined with lavish offices and conference rooms. The center was filled with different types of comfortable chairs and couches. Wilted plants and pots were scattered all through the center. This floor had beautiful American walnut hardwood. Greg whistled as he bent down to feel the dust-covered wood. The distinct swirled grain gave it a unique appearance.

Before the world stopped, Greg made his living at woodworking. He had various accounts where he would go and restore old homes or help create new homes that had woodwork. He had an ex-wife but no kids. All he left behind was a house because his wife took the dog. So after the world ended, he didn't have anyone to watch over but himself. This was probably the only reason he was alive.

Greg smacked the butt of his gun against the door and waited. He tried to slow down his breathing and listen. He listened for any noises that didn't sound right. Nothing happened. Greg repeated the motion. Waited. Nothing happened.

So he started to walk the entire floor. Nothing seemed out of place. It was like the floor was a snapshot in time. Nothing was askew. Not one thing. Not to mention the only prints in the dust were the cat's. Only the breakroom, in the center where the elevators were, had anything been moved around.

Someone at some point early on had moved a couch to the center where they sat and drank scotch. He figured someone had to have sat there and watched it all burn.

Greg was impressed with the rare bourbon selection behind the bar. He was also confused as to why there was a bar in an office building.

"This will come in handy someday, eh George?" he said as he bent down and took off his rucksack, and placed a bottle of Pappy Van Winkle 20 year into the large part of his pack.

George came strutting over at a quick pace. He rubbed himself up against Greg's shins and meowed.

"Yeah, I thought so too. Someday, this might be worth something to someone." Greg said as George just purred back at him.

In the large conference room on the south side of the building sat a large table with chairs. The chairs were a little out of place and papers were scattered around the tabletop. Each piece of paper warned the reader of some sort of virus outbreak and world-changing event. Each document had the MM Motors logo in the top right corner. They were all dated the day before the world ended. The rest of the floor was so perfect, it was like no one was even here on that horrible day.

"Know what, little guy? This would probably be a smart place to rest awhile," he said.

George meowed back at him.

"Yeah me too.," Greg responded. He moved back to a bar stool with a bottle of Lagavulin. After he carefully opened the bottle poured a finger's worth into a glass, and placed his nose over the rim. He inhaled deeply. The heavy smokiness and peaty aroma filled his nostrils. He paused briefly as he was taken back to a time with his ex-wife when they were happy.

The next morning, he was able to begin his search for car keys. Each floor took an entire day. He was very thorough. Each night, he slept on the 5th floor. Always on the same couch, and George would curl up on his chest. Once he gathered up all the keys he could find, he took them down to the parking lot.

All of the key fobs he collected worked. He was able to locate most of the vehicles without a problem. Greg checked each one he found. Slowly. Instead of just jumping in the first one that had the most gas, he moved his favorite choices to the building's entrance.

Back inside the building, Greg managed to rummage up some protein and granola bars. He grabbed some packets of instant oatmeal and piled it all inside his rucksack. Out of the entire building, he was able to locate four cans of unopened tuna. He snatched those up for George. After that, it was time to decide on transportation. They settled on a full-size Chevy van. This van had a full tank of gas and the inside was like a bedroom on wheels. Greg thought he could also live out of it for a bit too if he had to.

Greg and George ended up staying at MoGo Mato Motors for around two months. Greg would go out and scout during the day, then come back to the 5th floor at night. As usual, always cautious and always meticulous. This worked out for him for quite a while. Greg knew it wasn't safe to stay in one place too long. When the time finally came to move on, it made him a little sad to leave. They had called MoGo Mato Motors home for the short time they were there.

The van fired right up. Before putting it in gear, he let out an exasperated sigh.

"You ready furball?" Greg asked his feline companion.

George just ignored him and looked over the dashboard and through the windshield.

In the end, they drove off into the morning sun in their new conversion van.

TO BE CONTINUED...

THE END

www.ingramcontent.com/pod-product-compliance
Lightning Source LLC
Chambersburg PA
CBHW021404150726
47989CB00005B/2391